CRYPTID ISLAND

GERRY GRIFFITHS

SEVERED PRESS
HOBART TASMANIA

CRYPTID ISLAND

WWW.SEVEREDPRESS.COM

ISBN: 978-1-925840-44-5

DEDICATION

For my brother- and sister-in-law
Martin and Marlene
Paradise survivors of the Camp Fire

PART ONE

THE BOTANIST

1

THE RASH

Allen Moss' transformation was not caused by a radioactive arachnid's bite or exposure to a strange ocean mist, nor was it the result of a heavy bombardment of body-altering gamma rays or the consequence of crash landing on an alien planet. The change occurred when he innocently bent over one day and extracted a seemingly innocuous weed from the ground...

"So how long have you had this rash, Mr. Moss?" asked the dermatologist.

"I noticed it yesterday, after I came home from a job."

"What is it you do?"

"I have my own landscaping business."

"And where were you working?"

"Up in Los Alto Hills. My crew and I were clearing out some dense overgrowth for a customer."

"That area is notorious for poison oak."

"I know, but I rarely get it."

"Interesting. Does it itch?"

"No, it's more like a tingling sensation. Normally, I wouldn't have thought much of it but when I showed it to my wife, she said I better make an appointment and have it looked at."

"I see."

Allen took a deep breath. "It's not skin cancer is it?"

"No, I don't believe it's melanoma; at least not any case I've ever seen," the physician assured Allen.

Allen and the doctor took a moment to stare at the emerald swath on Allen's forearm. Its jagged, leafy edges covered an area six inches long and three inches wide.

"It does have an odd color," the doctor said.

"You don't think it could be one of those flesh-eating diseases they're always showing on those TV medical shows?"

"MRSA? That's an anti-drug resistant strain of staphylococcus, which is generally accompanied with red bumps or boil-like sores and a fever." The doctor glanced at Allen's medical file. "Your temperature was ninety-eight point six when you checked in, which is perfectly normal."

"So what do you think it is?"

"Probably an allergic reaction from the plants you were handling. Before you go home, stop at your local drugstore and pick up some over-the-counter zinc oxide ointment. Try applying it three times a day and see if that works. If the condition continues or worsens, come back and I'll prescribe something stronger."

"So, you don't think it's anything serious?" Allen slid off the examination table. He rolled down his shirtsleeve and buttoned the cuff.

"No, I think in a few days it should clear up."

"Thanks, doc," Allen said and left the examination room.

***

Allen strolled into the kitchen and stood behind his wife, Laney, who was working at the counter. He brushed her burgundy hair back and kissed her creamy freckled neck.

"You're home early," she said.

"I thought I'd let Carlos and the guys finish up today so I can catch up on some of the billing." Allen went over and opened the refrigerator. He peered inside. After a thorough perusal—even skipping the tempting six-pack of beer—he reconsidered and shut the door.

"I'm making your favorite."

Allen glanced in the mixing bowl. He saw the preparatory lump of ground turkey meat and dried breadcrumbs for meatloaf. He didn't have the heart to tell Laney that just the sight of the concoction made his stomach churn.

"So what did the doctor say?"

"Said not to worry. Told me this should clear it up." Allen pulled a small rectangular box out of a white pharmacy bag. "I think I'll go put some on."

"Dinner won't be for another hour."

"That's fine."

Allen went into the bathroom.

He unbuttoned his cuff, rolling up his sleeve. He removed the tube of ointment from the box. Twisting off the cap, he squeezed a worm-like bead along the spine of the rash. He smoothed the cream with the tip of his finger, covering the blotch entirely with a whitish coating.

He was putting the cap back on the tube when the patch on his forearm lit up like a fiery torch. "Jesus Christ!" He shook his arm to put out the invisible flame. “What the hell!” Allen never felt such pain. It was like someone jabbed his arm with a red-hot branding iron.

He twisted the spindle for the cold water all the way to the left, shoving his forearm under the faucet.

The water washed away some of the cream. His arm still burned. Frantically, he vigorously scrubbed his forearm until all of the ointment was gone.

Laney flew into the bathroom. “What’s wrong?”

“I don’t know. I think I had an allergic reaction to the cream. As soon as I put it on the rash it felt like my arm was on fire.” Allen kept his forearm under the running tap.

“Does it still hurt?”

“No, not now.”

“Let me see.”

Allen turned off the spigot. He grabbed a towel from the rack, dabbing his forearm. He held up his arm so Laney could see the rash.

“Kind of looks like one of those pine tree car fresheners.”

“Yeah, it does.”

“How does it feel now?”

“It still tingles. You know, this might sound strange but it’s like the rash didn’t want to be covered up.”

“Allen, that’s silly.”

“Yeah, you’re right. I better get some work done before dinner.”

***

“You haven’t touched your food.” Laney was unable to mask the disappointment in her voice.

“I’m sorry. I just don’t have an appetite.” Allen placed his unused knife and fork on the folded napkin by his plate of meatloaf and mashed potatoes.

“I worked so hard.”

“Maybe we can have sandwiches later.”

“Okay. How come you have your arm in your lap?”

“Promise you won’t freak out.”

“Allen, what’s wrong?”

“It’s spread.” Allen raised his arm and laid it on the table.

“Oh my God!”

“Don’t panic.”

“Allen! It’s taken over your entire arm!”

“It’s a little more than that.” Allen unbuttoned the front of his shirt, exposing his mantis green chest.

“Doesn’t it hurt?”

"Actually, the tingling sensation is almost pleasant."

"Allen, you're scaring me."

"I'm scaring *you*. How do you think *I* feel? I'm turning into the Jolly Green Giant!"

"We need to get you to the hospital!" Laney pushed away from the table. She was about to get up when Allen waved her back down.

"If the dermatologist doesn't know what it is, what's the point of going to the hospital?"

"Oh, Allen." Laney covered her mouth as tears flooded her cheeks.

"Honey, please don't cry." Allen got up. He went around to Laney's side of the table, putting his uninfected arm around her. "Don't worry. I'll be fine." He grabbed the pitcher from the table, chugging the water down to the last drop.

2

METAMORPHOSIS

"Something's come up, Carlos, and I need you to run things for a few days. No, everything's fine. You've got the schedule, so if you need help with anything, just give me a call. No, I'm not sure how long. Okay. Thanks. Talk to you later." Allen closed up his cell phone and laid it on the patio table.

The Moss' backyard was secluded with a six-foot tall redwood fence and plenty of shrubs, so there was no immediate threat of any of the neighbors peering over and seeing Allen shirtless, wearing only a pair of gym shorts.

His skin was asparagus green.

"How are you feeling?" Laney sat in a wrought-iron chair across from him. She had her laptop computer in front of her on the table, browsing different websites for information on what might be causing Allen's condition.

"The sun feels great." His eyes were closed, legs stretched out, basking in the sunlight.

Laney leaned forward. She watched the teal hairs on Allen's body undulate like grass swaying in a breeze, the tips straining up towards the sky.

As his wife, she should have been appalled. For some strange reason she wasn't sickened at all by the transformation. Something very bizarre was happening to Allen. It was up to her to help him figure it out. No matter what happened, Laney would never abandon him. "I have some theories," she said, astonished how Allen's skin was semi-hardening into what resembled the outside of a lime.

"What's that?" Allen reached down and grabbed the end of the hose. He put the spray nozzle over his head and gave himself a spritz. "Man, that feels good."

"You've turned green because for some unexplainable reason you have a high concentration of chlorophyll in your body..."

"So you're saying, I'm becoming some kind of plant-thing?"

"You don't believe me, look!" Laney reached over and stuck a sewing needle—one she appropriated from her basket strictly for the test—into Allen's hand, which apparently did not cause him any pain.

Allen opened his eyes. He glanced down at his hand. A jade liquid oozed from the pinprick.

"I have green blood?"

"That's right."

"Are you *serious*?"

"It's also why you have to keep hydrating yourself and the reason you crave sunlight so much. Your body is fueling up; getting its energy from photosynthesis. Which might explain your loss of appetite."

"I told you we could have sandwiches later," Allen quipped, but to be honest, he knew he couldn't eat a thing.

Laney read a few more facts on her laptop. "I don't know what's going on inside your body but I'll bet you're absorbing carbon dioxide right now and giving off oxygen."

"That's crazy."

"I'll prove it. Give me your arm."

Allen stretched his arm out. Laney poured her glass of water over it.

"If you look close, you can see tiny bubbles. That's oxygen coming out of your pores."

"That is amazing."

"How's your skin feel?"

"What do you mean?"

"Touch it," Laney said.

Allen felt the back of his right hand. "It feels prickly."

"Let me feel." Laney dabbed a finger on Allen's wrist. "Ouch!"

"What?"

"It's like getting poked by a stinging nettle."

"Well, that's not good."

"Sure it is. Your body's formed a protective shield. Like a plant would do, to keep insects off and animals away, so they won't eat it."

"What am I, a vegetable salad?"

"I want to try something." Laney picked up the newspaper on the table. She rolled it up into a cylinder.

"What are you going to do with that?"

"This!" Laney swung the rolled up newspaper, causing Allen to flinch, putting up his guard as she walloped him across the arm.

"Like that hurt," Allen smirked.

"You were ready for me." Laney looked down at the newsprint. "Jesus, Allen, look what you did!"

"What are those?"

"They're spines." A dozen three-inch long green spikes impaled the wadded newspaper.

"Those came out of me?"

"Nasty looking things wouldn't you say?"

"Awesome. Now I'm a frigging porcupine."

"You've devised your own defense system. Your skin's become super sensitive; air movement, barometric changes, any of that and your body reacts."

"Swell."

"Let's try—"

"Jeez, Laney, shouldn't you be careful? What if this is contagious?"

"Oh, crap. I got so excited, I didn't even think about that."

"Maybe we better sleep in separate rooms tonight."

"If I don't have it by now, I doubt if I'm going to catch it."

"All right, if you say so."

"But no sex, not until we know what we're dealing with, and I mean it."

3

CLOSE CALL

Allen awoke in the night, dying of thirst. “Laney, you awake?” Laney was in a deep sleep next to him, her back turned. Even though it was dark in their small bedroom, he could make out the outline of her slim figure; the dip of her side under her T-shirt, the curve of her hip, and the downward slope of her thigh and leg.

Not wanting to disturb her, Allen quietly slipped out of bed. He plucked the seat of his green plaid boxer shorts from the crack of his butt. He padded barefoot out of the bedroom and down the hall into the kitchen.

He opened the fridge. He took out a plastic bottled water.

Laney had left her laptop on the kitchen table with the screen flipped up. The power light was still on. Allen sat down at the table. He twisted the cap off the bottle, taking a deep swig of water. He pushed the enter button. The black screen illuminated the last website Laney had been consulting. He scanned the page, pushed the page down button to read some more. He was taking another drink when he saw an article making him almost choke. “Oh, no!”

Allen jumped up from the table. “Laney!” he yelled, running down the hall and into the bedroom. He flipped on the light switch. He rushed to the bed. “Laney, wake up!” he screamed, rolling her over and shaking her by the shoulders but her eyes wouldn’t open. He put his ear up to her mouth to see if she was breathing. Nothing. He shook her again. “Laney! Wake up!”

Laney didn’t stir.

Allen scooped his wife up in his arms. He carried her over to the bedroom’s sliding glass door, unlocking it. He slid the door open. He laid her on the back lawn. “Oh God, Laney breathe!” He placed his palms over her chest and began CPR. “Breathe, damn it, breathe!”

He wanted desperately to call 9-1-1. But what would he do when the responding paramedics showed up? How would he explain his appearance?

Allen kept pumping her chest. “Please, Laney—”

Laney opened her mouth, taking in a big hungry gulp of air like a hooked fish gasping on a boat deck.

"Thank God." Allen pulled Laney into a sitting position.

"What happened? Why are we outside?" Laney looked around somewhat bewildered.

"Something we didn't consider before we went to bed."

"What?"

"We didn't finish reading about photosynthesis. During the day, I'm converting carbon dioxide into oxygen, but at night, my body does the opposite. I was absorbing all of the oxygen out of the bedroom and converting it into carbon dioxide. I wasn't affected but you were running out of air. Laney, I almost killed you!"

"Honey, it wasn't your fault. We didn't know."

"We do now."

"These are precautions we need to be aware of." Laney smiled at Allen.

"My God, what's happening to me?"

"I don't know, but I'm a firm believer that everything happens for a reason."

A wet blob landed on Laney's thigh.

"Allen, are you crying?"

"I think so."

"I love you."

"Laney, I don't know what I would have done if something—"

"But it didn't," Laney reassured him. "Hey, if you carried me out here, how come my skin isn't irritated from you touching me?"

"I don't know."

"Wait a second; I think I do. I wasn't a threat to you, like when I swatted your arm."

"Are you saying what I think you're saying?"

"I think subconsciously, you can control this thing."

***

The following day it poured down rain and they couldn't go outdoors. It seemed especially gloomy inside the house. Allen was feeling depressed. When he first got up, he was a vibrant forest green. He sat at the kitchen table, watching Laney eat a bowl of bran flakes for breakfast. He still had no appetite for real food.

By late afternoon, he'd noticed his skin coloring had changed from dark green to a much paler shade, almost bordering on autumn brown.

"Looks like your batteries are running low. You need some sun," Laney told him.

Allen stood by the sink. He leaned on the counter in front of the kitchen bay window with two shelves of potted plants. He stroked the Boston fern's leaves.

Something remarkable happened: the plant's leaves turned brown as Allen's fingers became green. "Oh my God, are you seeing this?" Allen was jubilant as an explorer discovering a new land.

Laney stared in awe. "That's parasitic behavior. You're actually robbing the plant of its nutrients."

"So I'm killing it?"

"Yeah, stop that. I love that fern."

"Sorry."

***

The next day the rain stopped and the nourishing sun was ablaze. Allen took advantage of the warm weather. He spent the entire morning in the backyard, raking up leaves to recharge his batteries.

Not too long after, Laney opened the sliding glass door and called out, "Allen? Could you open this jar for me?" She glanced about the yard. Allen was nowhere to be seen so she went outside to look for him. She placed the jar of pickles on the patio table. She started to walk across the lawn. She tripped, falling on the grass. She immediately got to her knees, looking back to see what she had stumbled over. The garden hose was coiled up by the faucet.

Did she just hear footsteps?

She got up and brushed off her knees. "Allen? Where are you?"

Beyond the lawn, stepping stones led between hedgerows where Allen maintained a garden.

Laney started up the path only to find herself blocked by a barrier of brush. "What the heck? This wasn't here before."

"Hi, Laney."

"Allen?" Laney looked around the yard. "Allen, where are you?"

"I'm right here."

"Where? I don't see you..."

"I'm right in front of you."

Laney looked down at the hedgerow in front of her just as a portion of the brush rose in the shape of Allen and he became his visibly green self.

"Allen!" Laney cried out. "You scared the crap out of me!"

"Pretty cool, eh? I just learned I could do that."

"What in the world are you wearing? Is that a loincloth?"

"It's a fig leaf. Designed it myself. Extra large if you were curious."

"Dream on."

"Sorry about tripping you earlier."

"That was you?"

"Yeah. Check this out." Allen sat down on the grass and sprawled on his back. He blended in so well he was completely invisible.

"That's unbelievable. You're like one of those lizards that can camouflage themselves."

"You've got to admit, it's pretty incredible."

"I'll say."

4

SELF DEFENSE

"I have to get out of the house," Allen griped.

"Go out in the backyard."

"No, I mean *out*! Aren't you getting cabin fever?"

"Well, yeah. It would be nice to go for a drive or something," Laney had to admit.

"Let's go to the park."

"What, walk?"

"Sure, it's dark. No one will see us."

"What if someone does see you?"

"They won't. I think I'm getting a handle on this."

"It might not be too smart going over to the park at night."

"Come on, where's your sense of adventure?"

"Okay, but I still don't think it's a good idea."

***

Allen and Laney decided it was safe enough to go out just after midnight.

They kept to the shadows, avoiding the sidewalks en route to the park. Laney was wearing a black jogging outfit; Allen his manly fig leaf.

During the day, the family-oriented park was a place for older kids to shoot hoops; a small baseball diamond for Little Leaguers; an open meadow with picnic tables surrounded by eucalyptus trees, shrubs, and an old oak tree by the basketball courts.

At night, the park was a rendezvous for small-time dealers and drug addicts even though the local police frequently patrolled the neighborhood.

Allen and Laney crept between the trees like a pair of stealthy cats.

"I feel like a kid sneaking around," Laney whispered.

"Me, too." Allen placed his hand on the smooth trunk of a eucalyptus tree. He closed his eyes.

"What are you doing?"

"Shhh." Allen smiled then frowned; a look of shock came over his face.

"What's going on?"

"I'm having a history lesson."

"What?"

"My friend here is seventy-five years old. Did you know this park used to be an apple orchard?" Allen opened his eyes. He took his hand off the trunk.

"You're getting this from a tree?"

"I can't explain it. We just have a connection."

"So now you're the tree whisperer?"

"Apparently."

"Allen, you're—"

"Hey, are you assholes spying on us?"

Allen and Laney turned.

Two street punks stood by a picnic table, smoking weed. They wore T-shirts, denim jackets with cutoff sleeves, blue jeans, and motorcycle boots. The heavyset hooligan passed the glowing reefer to the taller bearded man. It was obvious they were looking for trouble.

"What do we do?" Laney whispered.

"Did you bring your cell phone?" Allen said.

"Yeah, it's in my pocket."

"Call the cops!"

The thugs charged across the picnic area.

"On second thought, *run*!" Allen yelled.

Allen and Laney dashed across the meadow toward the basketball courts.

"We have to hide." Allen dragged Laney behind the massive trunk of the oak tree.

The brutes converged on the tree. They stormed around the backside of the trunk, standing shoulder-to-shoulder like a couple of NFL linemen.

They stared directly at Allen.

Allen held his breath. He didn't move a muscle.

"Where'd they go?" said the heavyset bully.

"Hell, I don't know."

"You don't think they climbed up?"

"I don't see anyone up there."

"Christ, they must have doubled back on us. Come on, before they get away!"

Allen waited until he was sure they had gone. He stepped away from the trunk revealing Laney, who had been hiding behind him.

"Some trick, eh?" Allen said. "You squished behind me and me looking like the bark of a tree—it's the perfect disguise."

"Before your head swells into a watermelon, can we just go home?"

"Sure."

Allen and Laney took an indirect route to avoid any other undesirables that might be lurking on the outskirts of the park.

They were making a hasty retreat down the sidewalk when the heavyset thug jumped out from behind a shrub. He grabbed Laney.

"Hey, let her go!" Allen yelled.

"Will you look at the freak." The tall thug stepped out from behind the bush. "Gumby here looks like he's been snorting so much paint it's coming out of his pores."

"This isn't paint, you asshole."

"Who you calling asshole? Looks like someone should teach you some manners," the tall thug said. He raised his hand and there was a *snick* as the sharp metal shot out of his switchblade. With one quick motion, he lunged, slashing a deep gash down Allen's arm.

"Oh, my God!" Laney screamed.

"Shut up or I'll—"

Before the heavyset thug could harm Laney, Allen grabbed him by the throat with one hand. A thick, milky sap oozed out of Allen's fingers. The man gagged, his blue, swollen tongue flopping out of his mouth.

"Hey, let him go!" the tall thug shouted.

The heavyset thug's face turned bright red. He began to wheeze.

"Allen, you're sending him into anaphylactic shock!" Laney broke free from her attacker.

"What the hell are you, man?"

Allen released his hold on the heavyset thug and the man collapsed on the ground.

"You really want to know?" Allen looked down at the deep slash on his arm. He pressed one end of the sticky wound together with his forefinger and thumb. Like closing a zipper, he slid them down, sealing the gash as though properly suturing the wound, leaving no visible scar.

"You're a goddamn alien!" The tall thug fled down the sidewalk.

Allen stared down at the unconscious man, his face covered with hives. "You better call 9-1-1. I think I might have killed him."

Laney took her cell phone out of her pocket. She told the dispatcher a man was suffering a seizure near the park. She gave the location before closing her phone. "I'm pretty sure they'll be able to trace the call back to us."

"That doesn't give us much time. We better get home and pack," Allen said.

"And go where?"
"As far away from here as possible."

5

LORD OF THE JUNGLE

Brian Phillips had been trekking through the Amazon jungle for three days. His clothes were saturated from the humidity. The strap of his rucksack dug into his shoulder like a piano wire garrote. He was beginning to wish he'd never taken on the assignment, even though the editor of *Global Consortium News*, a watchdog publication, promised the photo/journalist a story worthy of a Pulitzer Prize.

Four hours ago, his guide refused to go any farther and left Phillips to hike on his own. The man had been frightened, babbling about evil spirits, further convincing Phillips the legend was true.

Phillips consulted the crude map with clandestine instructions that had been slipped under his hotel room door before deciding on the arduous journey. He continued down the narrow trail.

It was the middle of the day. The sun was blocked out from the two hundred foot Kapok trees canopy, the rainforest gloomy as a wet cave. He shuffled through organic matter and decomposed leaves, occasionally having to climb over a sprawling buttress root grown across the path.

The thick foliage teemed with white orchids and red and yellow flowered acacias. Every plant dripped, even though the torrential storm had long passed. Rainwater pooled in cupped bromeliad leaves. Philodendron roots descended from the treetops, searching for moisture; light-seeking epiphytes scaled the towering trunks in the opposite direction.

He heard spider monkeys chattering in the branches along with a background chorus of thousands of communicating insects. A bright yellow toucan squawked, poking its head out of a tree hollow. Tiny birds flittered overhead, swooping over the giant fronds. An ocelot yowled deep in the jungle.

Phillips sensed he was being followed. His suspicions were confirmed when he caught a glimpse of a small figure darting behind a blockade of stilt palms to his right. Then another appeared on his left. Soon, they were trudging just off the path, marching through the thicket, keeping pace with Phillips.

The trail led into a small clearing.

A woman was sitting on a fallen log. She wore a broad brim fedora shadowing her face, khaki shirt and pants, and brown boots. Twenty pigmy warriors stood behind her, armed with blowguns, and bows and arrows. More tribesmen watched from the high branches, while others peered out from behind the trees.

"Please, sit," the woman told Phillips. She pointed to a cut stump placed in front of the log.

The reporter walked over to the stoop. He unhooked the strap of his rucksack and sat down. He unzipped his bag. He removed a notepad and pen, and put them on his lap. He reached in again, taking out a digital camera with a long photo lens.

The pigmies immediately raised their blowguns to their mouths, archers pulling back on their bows.

The woman glanced over her shoulder. "They don't like cameras."

Phillips stuffed the camera back inside the rucksack.

"Thank you for making the journey to see me. Where is your guide?"

"He was too afraid to accompany me. I left him back on the trail."

"It was brave of you to continue on your own, Mr. Phillips."

"I've heard the Brazilian people are scared to venture into the rainforest because of an evil spirit that speaks to them, warning them to stay away."

"Only those that come to do harm."

"I believe they call it O Botanico."

"Yes, I am familiar with the name. Mr. Phillips, let me explain something to you. The Amazon region is an abundant resource, but, due to slash-and-burn practices, excessive logging, and decimating the jungle for agriculture and livestock, the rainforests are being destroyed. Did you know seventy percent of the three thousand variety of plants currently used to produce drugs to fight cancer are found here in the rainforest?"

"No, I didn't."

"Every day undiscovered plant species are forced into extinction due to deforestation. Plants lost forever, plants that might hold the cure to the disease. It is crucial these plants be saved. We just need more time to find them. That is why I summoned you here: so you can spread the word."

Phillips looked around at the stolid pigmies. All eyes were upon him.

"All right," Phillips said, picking up his pen and pad. "Where do we begin?"

For the next hour Phillips scribbled frantically, taking copious notes while the woman spoke.

The woman finished by saying, “That’s enough for now.”

Phillips gathered up his things, putting them in his bag. Standing, he shouldered the rucksack. He turned.

The trail leading back into the rainforest was no longer there as though it never existed. He became aware of the dead silence like the entire jungle was a waiting giant, patiently listening.

“Before you go, there is something you must see.” The woman got up. She walked over to Phillips, standing by his side.

Phillips saw the fear in the pigmy warriors’ eyes, and he too trembled.

“It’s okay! You can come out!” the woman called out.

For a moment nothing happened, and then, like a curtain lifting on an enormous stage, the rope-like lianas hoisted the drooping vegetation. The giant palms parted revealing the strange green man standing in the middle of the trail, his arms raised above his head like a maestro conducting an orchestra.

Phillips gasped.

“Mr. Phillips, I would like to introduce you to my husband, Allen Moss. The Botanist.”

6

THE DECIMATOR

Laney squatted behind a large fern and watched the massive piece of equipment down below move about the forest floor like an invading alien from another planet. The driver sat in an air-conditioned glassed-in compartment over the front section that maneuvered on dual treads much like a tank with an attached cargo bed, which had tall rail posts.

A large mechanic arm was attached to the center of the rig with a clamping claw at the end. It came down and fastened around the base of a tree. Laney heard the powerful saw blade cut through the trunk.

In mere seconds, the tree was separated from the ground, leaving hardly a stump, and hoisted in the air. The timber was fed through the apparatus, slicing off the branches, then halted. A ten-foot log was severed from the main tree and fell to the ground. Another section of tree was stripped of its limbs. Another log dropped onto the accumulating debris as the rest of the tree was processed.

The arm picked the logs off the ground and loaded them one by one onto the cargo bed.

Laney timed the cutting down of one tree. She was shocked to see how efficient and fast the process had been. Technological advances had eliminated the labor-intensive tasks of the logging industry with its computerized operations, meaning faster production and higher yields.

The thirty minutes it took to harvest 10 trees would take the same amount of years to replenish.

Laney raised a pair of binoculars to get a better look at the heavy equipment. She could see the operator inside the cab. He looked young, maybe in his mid-twenties, and had long hair and a beard.

She could see a familiar company logo on the side of the cab door and knew the powerful corporation had used its political muscle to gain unsustainable logging rights to the Amazon rainforest.

Laney looked down at the ground and spotted a large rock. She picked up the stone and cocked her arm, ready to throw.

A vine shot out of nowhere, wrapping around her wrist. “Hey,” she protested and spun around.

"Better not," Allen said. He released Laney, who dropped the rock. The vine retracted back into the index fingertip of his green-colored hand.

The humidity was high so he was hydrated and vibrant. His taut skin had the texture of the outside of an orange. His facial features were still Allen but his body had transformed into a chiseled human-shaped flora.

"You should've let me smash out his windshield."

"There's something you need to see. Follow me." Allen stepped onto a path between the trees.

Laney noticed, walking behind her husband, the vegetation near the trail reacted to Allen's presence like he was a famous celebrity maneuvering through an excited crowd of fans, everyone wanting to reach out affectionately to touch their idol.

Branches quivered and flower petals blossomed.

Creeper vines rose in salutatory waves.

The foliage ahead formed arches to welcome Allen.

Even though she knew it was only the shadows and the way sunlight filtered down through the canopy playing tricks on her vision, she still swore the trees swayed whenever Allen came in close contact.

He continued up a slope taking them to a ridge overlooking a small valley.

Allen leaned against a tree.

A leafy tendril on the bark caressed his neck.

"Stop that," he grinned, giving the trunk a playful pat.

Laney gazed down at the logging trucks and the large encampment of tents. "This is a major operation."

"That's not all. Look over there." Allen raised his green arm and pointed.

"Oh, my God!"

Ten heavy-duty tree-cutting machines were parked in a clearing; the same type as the piece of equipment she'd witnessed earlier.

7

VANDAL

As dusk approached, generator-powered floodlights began to turn on all around the perimeter of the sprawling campsite. While they waited for the sun to dissolve behind the trees, Allen stood on the ridge in plain sight, relaying what he saw to Laney concealed behind a mango tree.

"So far, I've counted maybe forty men and a handful of women going into what must be the mess tent." Allen wasn't afraid of being seen by anyone from down below as he blended into the backdrop of foliage behind him. It was like he was standing in front of a painting-in-progress and the artist had airbrushed over Allen's naked body, blending him into the landscape and making him virtually invisible; that is, until he moved and stepped away from the canvas.

"Do you see any guards?" Laney asked.

"Yes. There're three by the heavy equipment, another standing by the generators, and four or five roving the perimeters. By the looks of it, they're heavily armed. I'd say they're paranoid of being raided."

"I doubt if any of the indigenous tribes would be foolish enough to try and stop them."

"I agree. These guys look paramilitary." Allen stepped back and joined Laney on the ground at the base of the mango tree.

"So, what's the plan?" Laney asked.

"You stay here and—"

"I'm coming with you."

"I can't let you do that. It's too dangerous. I'm sure these guys have been instructed to shoot anything that comes within ten feet of their camp. I'll be better on my own."

"But who's going to watch your back?"

"You will."

"But how, if I'm stuck up here?"

"Give me a moment." Allen turned and placed his hand on the mango trunk. He shut his eyes, appearing to meditate.

After a few seconds he reopened his eyes. He looked at Laney. "If you think I might be in trouble, just give me a signal."

"And how do I do that?"

Allen half stood and grabbed an old tree limb off the ground. He handed the branch to Laney. "Strike the mango tree three times. But not too hard or you'll hurt it."

"And you'll hear that?"

"More like I'll feel it," Allen replied. "I know it sounds weird. We can figure it out later, when we have more time."

"Okay. I have to say, Allen, you never cease to amaze me." Laney stood up.

"I know, I'm an evolutionary wonder," he smiled. He tilted his head so he could clear the brim of Laney's fedora. He kissed her lightly, leaving a thin gloss of green pollen on her lips.

She ran her tongue over her upper lip. She sucked her lower lip into her mouth, savoring the residue of their kiss.

"Well, what's it taste like this time?"

Laney smacked her lips. "Would you believe, passion fruit?"

Since Allen's transformation, they'd been taking it slow, dreading his condition was contagious and they would never be able to share another intimate moment together. After a few indiscretions, they soon realized whatever drastically altered Allen wasn't transferable; at least not so far.

Allen gazed down at the brightly lit encampment below, accentuated by the surrounding nightfall creeping over the jungle like a black fog.

"Promise you'll be careful."

"Believe me, they won't even know I was there." Allen traipsed down the hill looking like a bizarre plant-thing that kept uprooting itself with each step. As he got closer to the tent city, he became more discreet, assuming the plant life around him to blend into his natural surroundings.

A patrolling guard walked by having no idea Allen was only an arm's length away, hugging a mahogany tree. As a joke, Allen willed an underground root to bulge up out of the dirt. The man stumbled and nearly fell. He turned around, staring at the ground. He saw nothing that might have tripped him up as the root had already receded back into the soil. The guard continued on his rounds.

Allen heard the clamor from the main tent as the work crews ate their meals and conversed loudly.

When he was near the generators, he made the mistake of stepping under the conical beam of a spotlight just as two guards came around the backside of a tent.

With no time to hide, Allen dropped to the ground onto his back in a patch of weeds. As the men approached, Allen shifted his body and moved his legs and arms evasively to avoid being stepped on, giving the impression it was their boots rustling the tall grass.

He rolled over onto his side and merged into the shadows.

Keeping to the trees, he snuck over to where the large tree-cutting machines were parked. They had tank-like treads for maneuvering over harsh terrain. Each harvester had a glassed-in cab reinforced with steel bars to protect the driver in the event of an accident.

On the back and side platforms were the propulsion engine and the motor for operating the mechanical arm that cut down and stripped the felled trees.

Allen jumped up, vaulting over a railing. He landed next to the cover housing the engine. He twisted the knobs on a side panel. He lifted the lid, exposing the intricate electrical wiring of the monstrous diesel engine.

He placed his hand on the manifold.

A black corrosive enzyme traveled from his fingertips onto the metal, spreading quickly over the engine, melting the insulated wires and plastic parts.

He closed the lid. He jumped down to the ground.

Allen crept to the next harvester, and symbolically, sabotaged the machine in the same amount of time it took for it to cut down a tree and make it into logs.

He continued on his mission, gutting one engine after another. He'd almost wrecked them all when one of the guards spotted smoke. Someone sounded a shrill ear-piercing alarm.

Allen posed in a cluster of ferns to watch the mayhem. More guards came running out of the tents, armed with assault rifles.

People started funneling out of the mess tent in a confused stupor.

Authoritative voices yelled in the night.

Spotlights traversed over the tent tops.

Allen nonchalantly slipped away, making his way up the incline to the hilltop.

Stepping around the trunk of the mango tree, he gloated, "They're officially out of business," expecting Laney to be there to greet him with open arms.

Laney was gone.

8

DETAINED

"Get your hands off me. Let me go," Laney protested as the security guard dragged her into the command tent. She tried to take a swing at him. He blocked the blow, shoving her to the ground.

"Where'd you find her?" asked a man wearing a black shirt and trousers with military-styled boots. A nine-millimeter semi-automatic pistol was on his right hip.

"Hiding on the ridge."

"I wasn't hiding, you jerk." Laney tried to get to her feet. The guard pushed her back down with his boot.

"Where are the others?"

"There's no one else. Just me," Laney snarled, glaring up at the man in charge.

"Let her up."

The guard reached down to help Laney. She knocked his hand away, getting up on her own.

"Was she armed?"

"No, sir."

"Go ahead, wait outside."

"Yes, sir." The guard stepped out between the tent flaps.

"What's your name?"

Laney refused to answer.

"All right. Then I'll begin. My name is Ivan Connors. I'm head of security for Wilde Enterprises."

"I'm still not telling you my name."

"Then tell me who you're working with?"

"You're wasting your breath."

"I want to know which activist group you're working for," Connors said, raising his voice.

Laney just stared at him.

"Fine. Have it your way." Connors grabbed her by the arm, marching her out of his tent. He turned to the security guard standing outside talking to another sentry. "You two follow me."

Connors escorted Laney roughly down a breezeway between the tents until they reached the area where the heavy-duty tree cutters were parked. The two guards took up positions a few feet away.

Laney could smell burnt rubber and a foul chemical odor, which made her cover her mouth with her free hand. She turned. Connors glared at her, motioning for her to look at the equipment.

"My job was to make sure nothing happened to these machines. Each one of these John Deere forwarders cost $250,000. Which means you destroyed two and a half million dollars worth of our property."

"I've seen what one of those things can do," Laney said. "Why so many?"

"We're a big corporation."

"And that gives you the right to destroy the rainforest?"

"A few trees aren't going to matter."

"You know, *we* will stop you," Laney said adamantly.

"So, I was right. You weren't acting alone. You'll be more cooperative when you're facing ten years in prison."

"You don't scare me."

Connors turned to one of the guards. "Put her in restraints. We're going for a ride." He looked at Laney. "I'm sorry, you leave me no other choice."

The guard slung his assault rifle over his shoulder. He reached into a pouch on his belt, taking out a set of plastic ties used for handcuffs. He grabbed Laney's left arm, tucking it behind her back.

"TAKE YOUR HANDS OFF MY WIFE!" a voice boomed from the jungle.

9

NIGHT RESCUE

When Allen stepped out of the trees, one of the guards gasped and raised his rifle.

The other guard looked at the man standing next to Laney. “What the hell is that? What do we do, Mr. Connors?”

“Shoot the damn—”

“Tell your men to put their guns down,” Laney yelled. “That’s my husband.”

“Your husband’s Swamp Thing?” one of the guards said.

Allen didn’t take offence to the man’s comment, as when he was a kid he’d liked the misunderstood comic book monster even though the grotesque creature was spawned from bog sludge instead of a luscious tropical forest. At the moment, Allen’s body was shingled with fern leaves and dotted with tiny purple flowers. Vines undulated about his body like starving stamens searching for food.

“Lower your weapons,” Connors ordered.

“That’s better,” Allen said.

“So it was you?” Connors said.

“That’s right. Would you mind releasing my wife?”

“And if we don’t?”

“That would be a big mistake.”

“Is that so?”

“Please, just let us go,” Laney pleaded. “He doesn’t want to hurt anyone.”

“What’s he going to do?” Connors grinned. “Give us a skin rash?”

“I’d listen to her if I were you,” Allen said.

“Words by someone that is about to become a tossed salad. Shoot the damn thing!”

The two guards fired shots.

Each slug passed through Allen’s body, ricocheting off the heavy equipment behind him. There was no pain, just the sensation of air ventilating through his torso. The bullet holes sealed instantaneously.

“You fools missed!” Connors yelled at his men.

A guard pulled a machete from the sheath on his belt. He charged Allen.

Allen raised his arm to stop the man. The blade came down, chopping Allen's hand off at the wrist.

Laney screamed.

The man took a step back expecting Allen to yell out with pain.

Allen glanced down at his bloodless stump. The hand magically formed right before everyone's eyes like a time-progression film of a plant growing in just seconds.

"Oh, you've got to be shitting me," a guard said.

"I'm telling you, stop, before someone really gets hurt," Allen warned.

"Then I suggest you back off." Connors put the muzzle of his pistol to Laney's temple.

Two more guards, hearing the gunshots, rushed into the small clearing. The four men stood protectively next to Connors with their weapons trained on Allen.

"Take him down and tie him up!" Connors shouted.

"I wouldn't touch him," Laney tried to warn them.

The first man yelped when he grabbed Allen by the arm. Razor-sharp thorns jutted through the man's palm and out the backside of his hand.

Allen blocked another attacker, seizing the man's face. When he removed his hand, the man's eyes, nose, and mouth were sealed tight by an adhesive sap. The man fell backward. A fellow guard caught him. He looked down in fright, watching the other man suffocate in his arms. Grabbing his knife from his belt, he slit the man's lips apart with the sharp blade. The man gasped, able to breathe, blood running down his chin.

Another guard rushed Allen.

Allen flicked his fingers and a milky goop splashed into his attacker's eyes, blinding him. He clutched his face, screaming, and stumbled back.

"Who's next?" Allen stared at the bewildered guards. He took a moment to glance around. He'd been so distracted by the scuffle he hadn't noticed that Connors and Laney were gone.

He heard a truck engine and spotted a Land Rover leaving the encampment.

The interior lights were on. He could see Laney staring back over the backseat, yelling his name as the vehicle sped off.

Allen shoved his way past the guards.

He ran after the vehicle.

He kept running, even as the red taillights faded into the jungle.

10

SHANGHAIED

The last thing Laney remembered was Allen standing there in the night; the mortified look on his face as he shrank from view. She had no idea where she was or how long she'd been riding in the backseat after being been whisked away as a cloth hood had been draped over her head shortly after leaving the encampment.

She could hear Connors whispering up front, giving the driver instructions. She squirmed, trying to free her hands bound behind her back. The insides of her wrists were pressed so tightly together she didn't have any wiggle room to loosen her restraints.

The vehicle slowed coming to a stop.

Laney heard the driver's door open. Connors got out on his side. She could feel a gush of cold air caress her exposed neck. She tasted the sea breeze on her lips when it wafted up under the hood.

The back door opened. Laney was dragged out.

She heard creaking wood and metal, water lapping against pilings, seagulls keening overhead, a not too distant foghorn.

A hand gripped the top of the hood, yanking it off with a few strands of Laney's hair.

"Hey!" She looked around the waterfront. They were standing on a pier at a shipping dock. She saw the driver leaning against the front grill of the Land Rover, remaining with the vehicle.

"Let's go." Connors guided Laney in the direction of a brow stretching up to the main deck of a merchant ship. She saw the gigantic letters WE on the side of the stack, the ship belonging to Wilde Enterprises, most likely the cargo ship that brought all the heavy equipment that was back at the logging camp.

They went up the gangway onto the main deck. Laney saw rows of twenty-foot long sea vans. She counted maybe fifty cargo containers.

The ship's captain and two crewmembers stood by an open hatchway leading through the bulkhead into the forward compartment.

"So who do we have here?" the captain asked.

"I want you to keep her locked up in one of your cabins until you reach the mainland."

"What?" Laney said. "You can't do this. That's kidnapping."

"Are you sure about this Connors?"

Laney could tell the captain wasn't too thrilled. She didn't like the way the two sailors kept leering at her; like they'd been out to sea so long they'd forgotten what a woman looked like.

"Don't worry. I'll have someone waiting to take her off your hands."

"So in the meantime, she's what...a prisoner?"

"Until she's properly charged."

"Don't believe him," Laney pleaded with the captain. "I had nothing to do with damaging that equipment."

"Maybe not you directly, but your husband did. Until we get him, I'm afraid it's all on you." Connors pulled a folding combat knife out of his trouser pocket. He flipped open the blade, slicing through the ties binding Laney's hands.

She slipped off the plastic straps, rubbing her wrists.

Laney saw Connors glance over at the two seamen still gawking at her. He directed his comment to the captain. "Tell your men if anything happens to her, they'll be dealing with me, personally."

The mariners looked at the captain with sly grins on their faces, thinking the man in charge of the ship had more authority.

"You heard him," the captain said sternly.

Their snickering smiles quickly waned into frowns.

"Take her below deck. Put her in the cabin next to mine," the captain told the two mariners. "Then alert the rest of the crew. Tell them we're about to get underway."

"Yes, sir."

"Wait, get your hands off me," Laney protested but the men were too strong and manhandled her toward the hatchway. She glanced over her shoulder. She saw Connors lean in to speak with the captain.

"There's a slight possibility her husband might try and—" he hesitated when he saw Laney watching him. He steered the captain away in the opposite direction.

Laney only managed to hear, "If he does, you'll have to set a..." and then they were too far away and she was forced inside the forward compartment.

11

THE TRAP

It hadn't been difficult following Laney's trail from the jungle to the wharf.

Whenever he *asked* if a vehicle had passed through a particular part of the rainforest, the vegetation around him had given a response only he could perceive so he could continue his pursuit in hopes of reaching Laney in time: much like following Hansel's trail of breadcrumbs.

Allen snuck inside a warehouse. He broke into a locker where a waterfront laborer stowed his gear.

It had been months since he'd worn clothes, but he thought it best, if he wanted to pass himself off as a dockworker on the pier. His feet felt constrained in the work boots and had already started to sprout through the leather, even bulging the tip of the steel-toed shoes.

He'd found a stevedore's jacket and had the hood up, concealing his face. Each time he crossed paths with another longshoreman, he would keep his head down, nod and mutter a greeting and keep on walking.

It was still dark. So far, no one suspected the strange man in their midst.

Allen ducked into the shadows.

A tall figure was coming down a brow, disembarking a ship about to pull away from the pier as Allen could hear the diesel engines idling through the hull.

Allen stayed out of sight, watching the man pass by.

It was the same man that had taken Laney.

Allen glanced up spotting the bold initials WE on the funnel and knew the cargo ship belonged to Wilde Enterprises. He couldn't believe Laney's abductor was leaving her on the ship, like a scallywag pirate snatching a coastal town wench.

The brow was about to be pulled up. Allen knew he had to act quickly and dashed across the pier. He jumped onto the gangway, clinging to the railing, as it was being hoisted in the air. He clambered up its length. He jumped down onto the main deck.

"What the hell you doing?" one of the sailors shouted, struggling with the ramp and having to drop it.

"Sorry, mate," Allen apologized, keeping his head down so no one could see his face. "Lost track of the time." He gave the men a dismissive wave and ducked through the hatch.

The narrow corridor was dimly lit, branching off into more passageways leading deeper inside the cargo ship. Every time Allen saw one of the crew, he would reverse direction or dart around a corner so as not to be seen. He wanted to call out Laney's name, hoping she might hear him and answer him back but then he would be giving himself away.

He stepped through a hatchway onto a catwalk overlooking a section of the engine room. Hot steam billowed up from the propulsion power plant.

Allen could feel his body absorbing moisture as it reacted to the humidity, his clothes clinging to him like damp washrags.

He dodged into another passage, which led to a gloomy cargo hold.

A foul smell assaulted his nostrils. He could see silhouettes of various sized animals moving about in small and large cages. The creatures reacted to his presence with snarls and anxious cries.

Allen continued on, reaching an apparent dead end. He climbed another set of metal stairs back up to the next level to an open hatch leading out to the main deck.

"Get your hands off me! Let me go!"

It was Laney.

Stepping through the oval hatchway, Allen followed the sound of his wife's voice. He dashed down a row between the tall cargo containers.

The front doors had been left wide open on a twenty-foot long sea van.

"Let me go!" could be heard deep inside the dark metal box.

Allen rushed inside, groping his way to the back. His hand touched the rear wall just as his boot kicked something on the floor. He reached down, picking up a flat device as it emitted, "Get your hands off me," from a tiny speaker.

"What the—?" Allen turned. A bright light shone in his face.

"Seems Connors was right about you," a man's voice said from behind the flashlight.

"Who are you? Where's Laney?"

"I am Captain Millry. You have illegally boarded my vessel. Therefore, you must be detained. Close the doors."

"No, he'll die in there," Laney shouted from outside.

“LANEY!” Allen yelled. He bolted toward the light. The heavy doors swung shut, locking him inside.

12

HIGH SEAS

Allen wasn't certain of the precise time. He knew it was daylight outside as a thin shaft of sunlight was shining into the dark shipping container through a dime-size rust hole just above his head.

Reaching up, he'd extended a three-foot long tendril of himself through the chink, which stood erect like a radio antennae; instead of receiving a transmission signal, the sapling was soaking up sunlight so Allen could convert light energy via the photosynthesis process into organic fuel.

He'd considered threading himself gradually through the vent to escape but wasn't sure of the outcome or if he would even be able to reform back into his original shape, as he had never attempted it before. He decided to leave the option as a last resort.

The garments he'd been wearing were on the container floor. He had absorbed every drop of moisture from the damp clothes. It was necessary to allow his body to breathe freely.

He wasn't too worried about the lack of water or sunlight. He figured the egress would allow him to put enough of himself on the rooftop of the shipping container to sponge up the wet sea air and absorb the sun's rays.

Allen was more concerned about Laney. He knew his wife was smart and resourceful. He feared for her safety in the company of the unscrupulous sailors.

As none of the crewmembers had gotten a good look at him, they had to assume he was like anyone else and in time would require provisions. There was nothing Allen could do at the moment but wait for someone to open the steel doors so he could stage an escape and rescue Laney.

And that is exactly what he did.

He sat in the corner of the shipping container—and waited.

***

For two days, Laney was confined to her quarters and not permitted to leave the cabin. The captain had paid her a visit to check in on her. When she demanded to be released and reunited with her husband, the captain assured her they would once they reached port.

A ship's steward brought Laney her meals, which consisted mostly of longanisa and rice, chicken adobo, or lumpia. Whenever she tried to get information out of him, the short Filipino man would give her a toothless grin and shake his head like he didn't understand her, though she had heard him speaking perfect English in the passageway to the sailor standing outside, guarding her door.

Laney was taking a nap when her compartment tilted suddenly, tossing her out of her bunk. She flew across the room, slamming into the small table by the bulkhead. The floor heaved in the other direction and she was thrown against a metal cabinet.

The room pitched forward and then back, throwing her off her feet. It was like trying to stand up in a roller coaster car as it barreled into steep turns, thundering up and down the tracks.

She heard the lock click. Her cabin door swung open.

"Hurry, come with me!" yelled the sailor. He held onto the doorjamb, reaching out to Laney.

She stumbled across the floor. She grabbed his hand. "Where are we going?"

"Topside."

"Why, what's happening?"

"We've hit a bad storm." The sailor staggered down the passage, banging up against the bulkhead as he held onto Laney. Each time the ship lurched violently, the hull around them groaned, followed by pounding booms from the outside waves.

They clung to the railing, climbing up the steel stairs to the upper deck. Seawater splashed in through the open hatchway, drenching Laney and the sailor.

Stepping outside, Laney could see the giant white caps on the rolling waves, some higher than the top lip of the ship's funnel. The bow plunged and the vessel dipped into a deep trough like the sea was swallowing them up.

As the winds howled and the waves crashed onto the main deck, rivers of saltwater gushed between the cargo containers like a flashflood rushing through a city's streets.

Laney spotted the captain and a few of the crew preparing to launch a lifeboat.

She turned to the man next to her and shouted, "Are we abandoning ship?"

"There's been a breech in the hull," he replied, ducking as another powerful wave slammed into the hull, sending a raging torrent across the main deck.

Laney clung to a cleat on a mast to stop from being swept overboard as the ship drastically tilted in a 45-degree angle. She was certain the ship was going to capsize but it slowly uprighted and began to lean the other way.

She heard muffled screams and saw the captain and his men being swept over the side into the choppy sea.

Suddenly, the cargo ship rose on the crest of a mammoth sixty-foot wave. She heard a thunderous boom then a giant crack split the main deck apart. "Oh my God!" Laney screamed.

"That monster wave broke the ship's back," the sailor shouted, holding onto a halyard on the other side of the mast. "We have to get to the lifeboat!"

Laney watched in horror as the bow section separated and drifted into the turbulent sea. The shipping cargo containers slid against one another but managed to stay with the damaged vessel.

Her heart sank knowing Allen was trapped with no way to get out. She watched as the ravaged section floated further away. Some of the compartments on the different levels appeared to be sealed. She prayed there was enough buoyancy to keep the wreck afloat until help could arrive.

"We're going down!" the sailor hollered.

Laney had been so preoccupied worrying about Allen, she hadn't realized the stern section of the ship was rapidly sinking.

"We have to go!" The sailor grabbed Laney by the hand. They staggered like a couple of drunks as the deck shifted and waves crashed over them. As soon as they reached the open lifeboat, the sailor boosted Laney aboard.

She watched as he struggled to release the block from the tackle clamping down on the rope suspending the boat. The sailor gave it a strong yank. He lost his balance. He fell over the side, plummeting into the ocean.

Laney looked up as the block gave way. The rope raced through the pulley, dumping the small whaleboat into the rough sea.

She knew she needed to get clear of the sinking vessel before it sucked her down with it. She spotted a set of oars. She rigged them in the holders.

Sitting on the bench seat and facing aft, she dipped the paddles in the water. She put her shoulders into it and rowed like her life depended on it.

The stern section of the ship stood on end. Air bubbled out from the hulking metal as it began to submerge, creating a powerful whirlpool.

Laney could feel the lifeboat being drawn toward the swirling current.

Leaning forward and pulling back with all her might, she rowed as hard as she could and kept doing so, until the boat finally broke free of the undercurrent threatening to suck her under with the doomed ship. She gazed over the gunwale hoping to see at least one other survivor in the water, but it was too dark.

Praying the lifeboat was seaworthy to ride out the storm, Laney crawled under the canvas tarp stretched over the bow and curled up with a life preserver.

13

ADRIFT

By the afternoon of the next day, the ocean waves had subsided as the storm had dissipated and moved southward. There were no sightings of a ship or land anywhere on the horizon. The sky was a magnificent cloudless blue dome.

Laney felt as though her entire body was bruised from being slammed against the inside of the hull for all those hours. She had pulled everything out from under the canvas tarp in the process of conducting an inventory.

Besides the life jacket she was wearing, there were five more. If the lifeboat was to sink, and the need arose, she could tie the life preservers together to form a crude raft.

A single bucket was useful for scooping up tiny fish and bailing water, and would make for an adequate latrine.

She looked inside the waterproof green bag labeled with the ISO first aid symbol of a white cross. It contained standard medical supplies: adhesive bandages, tape, gauze pads, disposable nitrite gloves, butterfly closure strips, alcohol swabs, hydrogen peroxide, anti-seasickness tablets and a tube of UV protection ointment. She applied the sunscreen to her face and arms to prevent her fair skin from becoming sunburned.

Laney wore a khaki sun hat she'd found tucked in the bow to ward off the scorching sun. She'd donned a pair of sunglasses from the kit to protect her eyes from the water's glare, which could result in blindness much like staring for long durations with the naked eye at a white landscape of snow.

She had a compass but no idea which way was the nearest shoreline.

Inside an orange box was a flare gun with two red flares and two smoke flares. She had never shot a flare gun before. After reading the straightforward instructions on the side of the box she felt she was prepared to fire a projectile in the event she sighted land or a passing ship.

She was disappointed the lifeboat didn't have a distress beacon, a shortwave radio, or a GPS navigation device, which would have increased her chances of being rescued.

Laney was confident she had ample food. A cardboard box contained cans of high-calorie rations—and thankfully a can opener—enough provisions to last six people for one week or one person for six weeks. A small block of chocolate was wrapped in aluminum foil to contain the confection if it melted.

She'd discovered a seawater desalination kit and a rainwater-collecting device. She wasn't overly worried about running out of water right away as there were 6 one-gallon jugs on board.

She also had a foul weather poncho, a waterproof flashlight, and a Swiss Army knife.

Laney stowed everything that needed to be out of the sun back under the bow tarpaulin. She grabbed the block of chocolate. She used the Swiss Army knife to cut herself off a piece. She put the sweet bit in her mouth, resting it on her tongue. She allowed it to slowly dissolve and slide down her throat.

Afterwards, she took a Dramamine. She washed it down with a swallow of lukewarm water from a jug. She slipped under the shade of the tarp. She closed her eyes, letting the gentle rocking of the boat lull her to sleep.

***

The boat shook with a loud boom.

Laney woke up, scrambling out into the bright sunlight. She removed her sunglasses from her shirt pocket. She put them on.

The boat was swaying roughly so she had to grab the gunwale so as not to fall over. She could hear water lapping against the hull.

She peered over the side. She didn't see anything in the water the lifeboat might have hit. Sitting on the bench seat, she turned halfway around to her right. She turned back the other way to make a complete 360-degree sweep. All she saw was a colossal circle of flat ocean.

Something bumped the keel. The stern lifted up, bouncing back onto the surface. Laney grabbed onto the oar holder to stop from being thrown out of the boat.

This time when she looked over the side, she saw a humongous dark shape pass beneath the boat. Laney estimated the lifeboat to be sixteen feet in length. The great white shark was nearly twice that size.

The deadly predator swam just below the surface. It headed away from the boat.

A minute later, the triangular-shaped dorsal fin emerged a hundred yards out, cutting back through the water toward the lifeboat.

Laney pulled an oar out of the holder. She crouched with the paddle ready. She figured if she could bash it in the head, the great white might back off and leave her alone. She waited as it made its next pass. She raised the oar and jabbed at its face through the water.

The shark opened its mouth, grabbing the oar in its serrated teeth. Fearing she would be pulled over the side, Laney released the oar. The 4-ton beast plunged into the blackening depths.

Laney cursed herself for being so stupid. It would be near impossible to maneuver the lifeboat with only one oar. Instead of dissuading the mighty fish, she had only provoked it. Now she had given it a real reason to attack.

The great white punched through the planked hull with its head like a silver bullet ripping through a paper target.

Laney fell back against the transom. Water rushed into the boat through the three-foot wide gap left from the smashed-out boards. She watched in horror as her survival gear floated out with the jugs of water. The case of canned goods sunk right away.

"No, no!" She lurched over the bench seat, grabbing for anything before it slipped out into the open water. She snatched the orange case containing the flare gun.

She stood in the boat. The water level had reached her knees. She was sinking fast. She removed the flare gun from the case. She inserted a red flare.

The great white shark was circling back to the boat.

White Death in a sea of blue.

Water poured over the transom.

The shark came alongside—opened its monstrous mouth.

Laney aimed and fired.

Red phosphorus burst out of its cavernous gullet.

The massive creature rolled onto its back and slowly sank.

Laney put the flare gun back in the waterproof case.

The lifeboat was completely filled with water. Laney jumped in, swimming toward the life vests. She gathered them up before they could drift away. She cinched them together forming a larger flotation device. She was able to grab a water jug as it floated by.

An hour ago, she had high hopes of survival; now, not so much.

***

Laney drifted for days on the ocean currents before Butros Jabeen and his crew spotted her some miles off the coast of Madagascar. She was dehydrated, suffering from hypothermia, and her body had tiny bites all over where the fish had tried to feed on her.

She counted her lucky stars to be alive.

As did the pirates that rescued her.

14

BLOOM

Allen stood on the shipwreck, staring at the barren island. Stone beaches stretched up to sloping ridges of black lava rock. Hot vapors steamed up from the earth's crust in a rising gray plume out of the conical mountainous peak.

The portside bow section of the ship's hull was crushed against the shoreline boulders, along with a few shipping containers. Most of the twenty-foot long sea vans had slid off the deck, visible in the surf or resting on the ocean's bottom.

Allen's container was the only one still on the main deck.

The doors stood wide open, exposing the interior of the metal box, which was lined with moss-green fungus and bulging with plant life. The overgrown vegetation's budding root systems had expanded onto the main deck, creeping into every crack and crevice. Thick vines slithered through portholes and hatchways, wrapping around railings and stanchions like a conquering invading army of serpents.

Allen glanced down at his chest, legs, and feet. He was amazed by the way his body had changed once he'd been exposed to plenty of sunshine and the moist sea air.

When Allen first stepped out of the shipping container, he looked like he had been dipped in a sticky substance and rolled in corn flakes from head to toe. When he touched his brittle skin, pieces would crack off like autumn leaves falling off a tree.

But now his humanistic body was covered with a bouquet of tiny purple flowers and white baby breath.

He heard scampering feet. Another animal had escaped from the cargo hold making its way off the wrecked ship onto the boulders to the stony beachfront.

A bird glided down to perch on Allen's shoulder like a pirate's parrot.

It was a tern.

Allen could hear soaring gulls gibbering high up in the sky.

He turned his head. The small bird was staring at him. It bobbed its black skull capped head, clacking its orange beak to greet Allen.

"Well, hello there," Allen smiled. He watched as the bird's white body and wing feathers slowly began to dapple into fuzzy, purplish speckles.

Amazed by the bird's transformation, Allen wondered if he was forming a mutualism relationship with the bird.

The tern chirped excitedly, flapping its wings like an animated Disney cartoon character.

Allen held his right arm straight out from his side.

Two gulls landed on what may have appeared to them as a tree branch. Their plumage instantly began to sprout tiny gypsophila flowers. It was evident Allen's condition was transferable to other creatures merely through touch. He hoped it wouldn't prove to be a bad thing like being exposed to poison oak or something deadly.

He watched with trepidation as the two birds turned into floral sculptures.

Allen jiggled his arm. He was relieved when the strange-looking gulls flew off.

He climbed over the deck railing. He jumped onto a boulder. He made his way over the rocks until he reached the gravelly beach, stepping onto the lava-formed island.

He took a few steps then looked back at what looked like footprints in the sand, though he had been treading on solid rock—a mossy trail shaped by the soles of his feet.

Moss began to spread in all directions like a gentle flood, filling each rock pore with newborn life. Fungal spores drifted up to higher ground on the incoming ocean breeze giving birth to millions of tiny toadstools on the hillsides and setting the stage for things to come.

Allen spread his arms apart like a prophet and gazed up at the transforming landscape. He turned to smile at the splendid bird on his shoulder. "Welcome my little friend to Cryptid Island."

PART TWO

THE CRYPTID HUNTERS

15

HAWE

Jack Tremens and Miguel Walla followed the two heavily armed park rangers through the trees into the tall grass. They'd been on foot for the past twenty minutes after leaving the rangers' Land Rover on the other side of a large boulder not too far away from an old flatbed truck they'd discovered concealed in a grove of umbrella thorn acacias.

For three months, Jack and Miguel had been conservational stewards volunteering their services. They had been assisting Dr. Karl Hiller and his wife, Cynthia, both compassionate and skilled veterinarians who had recently established Hawe Wildlife Preserve: Hawe being the African word for haven. The sanctuary was almost 200 square miles in the savanna plains and was an extension of a bordering national park.

The Hillers' mission plan was to provide proper medical assistance to endangered species and protect the wildlife from poachers.

The atrocities Jack and Miguel witnessed while working on the reservation were enough to turn anyone's stomach. The needless slaughter of mutilated animals left to rot in the sun while poachers made a bleak living peddling rhino horns to be ground up for aphrodisiacs and elephant tusks to be carved into tourist trinkets, leopard skins to clothe egocentrics in exotic furs, and any other animal byproducts illegally sold on the Black Market.

With so many animals roaming such an expansive area, it was an impossible job ensuring their safety from unscrupulous poachers who were not unlike heartless looters swooping in unexpectedly and raiding homes during a forced disaster evacuation.

No animals were exempt from the poacher's greed, even if it was just for the meat. The amount of species going extinct everyday was staggering. Jack and Miguel hoped to somehow turn the tide.

"How many?" Jack asked.

"I count six separate footprints," Amare said, glancing over his shoulder. The park ranger wore a beige safari hat, military fatigues, and was armed with an M4 carbine.

Haji, the other ranger walking beside him, was similarly dressed and carried the same style weapon.

"Shouldn't be a problem," Miguel replied, giving Jack a wink.

Jack drew a bandana out of his back pocket and mopped his forehead. The center of his shirt between his shoulder blades was soaked from the torrid African heat.

As the two park rangers were carrying assault rifles with 30-round clips and were combat trained, Jack and Miguel only wore side arms. Jack had his Colt .44-magnum revolver holstered on his right hip, Miguel a Desert Eagle .357 semi-automatic pistol in a shoulder rig. They had their five-inch serrated blade hunting knives sheathed on their belts if needed.

They'd been traipsing through the tall grass for maybe five minutes when Amare raised his right arm in an L-shape and made a fist. He glanced over at Haji, pointing straight ahead.

Jack heard voices up ahead. He drew his gun, holding it down by his thigh. He looked over at Miguel. His pistol was out of the holster.

The men stepped out of the high grass into a dirt clearing.

Five African men in shabby clothes had their backs turned to them. They were spread out around a giant thirty-foot tall termite mound. The poachers were kicking and using the butts of their guns like brooms, trying to move armored anteaters away from the termite hill.

The animals were pangolins, the most desired species for illegal trafficking as their meat was considered a delicacy. Their keratin scales were used for medicines, and because of that, the timid animals were being hunted to extinction.

Jack watched an anteater roll itself up into a protective ball. A poacher reached down with his bare hands to pull it apart. He screamed suddenly as the sharp scales tore into his flesh.

Another poacher snuck up behind a pangolin. The animal raised its scaly tail, spraying him in the face like a skunk. The man stumbled back, rubbing furiously at his eyes. He slammed the butt of his rifle down on the pangolin's tiny head, crushing it into the dirt.

"Put down your guns!" Amare yelled, aiming his carbine at the poachers.

Haji pointed his weapon at the man with the bleeding hands.

The other poachers stared indecisively at the park rangers.

Jack moved to Amare's side.

Miguel stood next to Haji.

They kept their side arms pointed at the ground so as not to provoke a gunfight.

Studying the five poachers, Jack gave Amare a sideways glance and whispered, "I thought you said there were six?"

"There are," Amare replied.

The unaccounted-for poacher stepped out from behind the termite mound with a single-barrel shotgun and fired.

Amare yelped as the buckshot peppered his left side, some of the stray pellets striking Jack in his right arm.

Haji let out a short burst of machinegun fire, cutting down the shooter. The other poachers raised their gun muzzles.

Jack shot the man with the bleeding hands, reaching into his waistband to draw a vintage pistol. The magnum slug punched a hole in the man's forehead the size of a silver quarter.

Miguel blasted the poacher that had killed the pangolin. The man dropped his rifle and slumped to the ground beside the dead anteater.

A machete-wielding man charged Jack. He raised his revolver to block the blow as the blade came at his face. His gun was knocked out of his hand. The poacher swung again. Jack ducked. The broad sword swished over his head. Jack extended his left hand, burying the sharp steel of his combat knife into his attacker's upper leg. He yanked out the blade. The man collapsed to the ground, blood gushing out the wound.

Two poachers threw down their guns. They raised their hands high in the air.

Haji stepped towards them. He aimed his carbine at a poacher's head.

"Haji!" Amare shouted.

The park ranger ignored his wounded cohort.

"Do not do that!"

Haji glared at the trembling poacher. He began to lower his gun. He brought the stock of his assault rifle around, striking the man across the face, sending him sprawling onto the dirt. "You, on the ground!" he snapped at the other man.

When they were facedown on the sun-baked ground, Haji stood over the prone men. He handcuffed them with plastic ties.

Jack watched as more pangolins came out of nearby burrows, heading toward the termite mound. Some of the long-tailed aardvarks took a couple of bipedal steps before walking on all fours.

The animals converged at the base of the huge termite hill, flicking their long tongues inside the loose soil, searching for tasty insects.

Miguel watched the pangolins going about their normal routine as though nothing had happened. "It's lucky we came along."

"Tell that to them," Jack said, gazing down at the dead poachers.

***

"You were fortunate it was only birdshot," Dr. Hiller said, dabbing blotches of antiseptic ointment on Jack's arm. Amare was sitting on the edge of a gurney with his feet dangling over the edge. His side had been taped up and he was putting on his shirt.

"So I imagine those poachers will be locked up for some time," Jack said.

"I wouldn't count on it," Dr. Hiller said.

"What do you mean?"

"Most times poachers aren't even convicted or pay only a small fine."

"That's ridiculous. And why's that?"

"Because our judges are too lenient," Amare said, hopping off the gurney. "If I were a judge, I would send every poacher to the gallows. String them up and be done with them. Let them go and they just go out and kill more animals."

"It doesn't seem right," Jack had to admit. "There should be stiffer laws."

"I agree," Dr. Hiller said. "But you have to remember for some of the local people, poaching is their only source of income where wild game is considered a free resource."

"What about government intervention?"

"There is too much corruption."

"Surely, there has to be an answer."

"There is. We continue our efforts protecting these animals and hopefully in time more sanctuaries like this one can be created and national parks will be allowed to expand. But of course, that would require additional government funding," Dr. Hiller said with a pained look.

"In other words, don't hold your breath," Jack said.

"Exactly." Dr. Hiller patted Jack lightly on the back. "You were lucky the pellets barely penetrated the skin." The doctor turned to Amare. "You, on the other hand, better see me in the morning so I can change your dressing."

"Thank you, Dr. Hiller," Amare said. He gave Jack a wave and left the examination room.

Dr. Hiller looked at Jack. "Well, I have a sick vulture to attend to."

"Thanks for patching me up," Jack said and walked out of the room. He strolled down the long corridor and went outside.

He ambled past the corrals and the stucco animal enclosures behind the treatment clinic. He saw volunteer villagers that traveled up to ten miles a day on foot roundtrip, feeding and taking care of injured animals.

Haji was standing guard in front of a lion cage where the poachers were being held, awaiting transport to the nearest jail.

Cutting across the open yard, Jack went up to a cottage porch. He knocked on the door.

"Come in," a woman's voice beckoned.

Jack opened the door, stepping inside.

"Aren't they the cutest things ever?" five-year-old Sophia beamed, kneeling next to a cardboard box filled with a litter of six wild dog pups. They looked like canine Musketeers with their comical oversized ears. Their mishmash hides were a tapestry of different earth tone colors.

"I'll say," Jack replied.

"Cynthia brought them over for Sophia to play with," Maria said, sitting in a chair beside her daughter so she could supervise playtime.

"Where's that husband of yours?"

"Sitting out on the observation deck with his computer."

Sophia squealed.

Jack saw all six puppies standing on their hind legs with their front paws on the lip of the cardboard box, slobbering Sophia's hands with their tongues.

"Better be careful they don't lick you to death."

Sophia giggled until one of the pups nipped her hand. "Ouch, stop that!"

"See, I told you," Jack laughed. He stepped through the room to the sliding glass door leading out to a wooden deck overlooking a small lake and the sprawling savanna stretching for miles to the mountain range on the distant horizon.

Jack closed the sliding glass door behind him to keep out the heat. He went over to the picnic table where Miguel sat, typing on the keyboard of his laptop.

"Updating our blog?"

"I just posted a short account of what happened today." Miguel looked up from the screen. "You should be happy to know we've reached a new milestone and have almost 3,500 followers."

"That is good news." Jack sat on the bench across from his friend. He gazed out at the panoramic view.

"I'm thinking of making some web design changes." Miguel pointed at their homepage, which had caricatures of Jack and Miguel. There was a strong resemblance to their faces but their bodies were more cartoon-like. Jack was the tall, buff, action-type explorer, while Miguel was shorter and partially obscured, peering out from behind a tree like a buffoon.

"Why, what's wrong with it?" Jack asked.

"Maria says I look like Bernardo."

"Who's Bernardo?"

"Zorro's sidekick."

"That's crazy," Jack said. "I look nothing like Zorro."

"Changing the subject, ever heard of a Professor Nora Howard?" Miguel asked.

"Can't say as I have."

"It seems she's been taking a special interest in our website, writing comments and requesting we get in contact with her."

"Really. Any idea who she is?" Jack asked.

Miguel tapped a key and turned his laptop around on the table so Jack could see the screen. "Here she is on Google."

Jack took a moment to read Nora Howard's biography. She was raised in Montara, California and had earned her PHD at Stanford University, majoring in bioengineering and had graduated with various honors in programs researching cloning, stem cells, and cellular biology. She enjoyed hiking and traveling and had an unaccredited metaphysics degree in Cryptozoology. She was currently employed at Wilde Enterprises.

There was also a picture of her to the right of the article. She was an attractive blonde with piercing blue eyes and a cute smile.

"Pretty. For an egghead," Jack quipped.

"I think she wants to hire us."

"Hire us for what?"

"Not completely sure."

"Can you contact her?" Jack asked.

"Sure. Let me shoot her an email."

***

They had just finished eating dinner outside on the deck when Miguel's laptop chimed, signaling an incoming email. It was a three-pager from the professor, outlining her proposal with attached contractual agreements.

Jack and Miguel read the email twice as it seemed too unbelievable.

"This is a hoax, right?" Miguel said, sitting back from his computer. He glanced through the closed sliding glass window at Maria standing in front of the kitchenette sink, washing the dishes while Sophia sat at a small table, drawing pictures of the animals she'd seen that day.

"Pretty wild, that's for sure. That company the professor works for must have money to burn, seeing what it's willing to pay us."

"*If* we deliver the goods," Miguel said. "Let's say for a second that this is on the level and we agree to sign up. I'm not sure I want Maria and Sophia coming along."

"You're right. Some of those places mentioned in the email look pretty dangerous."

"Do you think the Hillers would mind if Maria and Sophia remained here?"

"I don't see why not. They can always use the help. But will Maria go for it?"

"She will. Once she sees what these people are willing to pay us."

"It might mean being away from them for stretches at a time. You saw the itinerary the professor had planned for us."

"True, I'll miss them but think what we can do with the money. Definitely boost our online presence and spread the word about endangered wildlife."

"I'm game if you are."

"Then I guess we're doing this?"

"Pull up those contracts."

Miguel returned to his computer. He clicked on the blue attachment. "I'm definitely changing our homepage." He looked at Jack and struck a pose like he was mugging for the camera. "What do you think? Antonio Banderas? Jimmy Smits?"

"In your dreams."

16

MNGWA

The Cessna 340A made its descent, touching down on a field near a small village nestled at the base of a grassy hill.

"This is it," the pilot yelled back. The twin engines whined down, each propeller coming gradually to a stop.

When Jack and Miguel were picked up from Hawe Wildlife Preserve, they weren't told their destination. Looking out the windows, they knew the general direction was south by the position of the sun.

From the passenger compartment, Jack had watched the pilot in the cockpit taking flight instructions over his headset. Every so often the pilot would make a slight correction, altering their course.

"And where are we exactly?" Jack asked the pilot as he stepped from the cockpit and came down the aisle. Instead of the traditional captain's uniform, the bush pilot was wearing a polo shirt with a WE emblem above the shirt pocket, a pair of slacks and dress shoes.

"Tanzania."

"That's pretty broad," Miguel said.

"Sorry, but that's all I can tell you."

Jack knew by the pilot's tone they weren't going to get any specifics.

Miguel's laptop chimed on the seat next to him. The pilot took it as his cue to return to the cockpit.

Miguel raised the cover, putting the laptop on the pull down food tray mounted to the back of the seat in front of him. He saw Professor Nora Howard on the screen, sitting behind her desk, wearing a white lab coat.

"Hi, Miguel. I take it Jack is with you?" The professor clasped her hands together on the desktop.

Jack leaned over from his seat so he could be seen by the camera aperture on the top of the computer, placing him in the frame with Miguel in the lower right hand corner of the screen. "Do we call you professor or Nora?"

"Nora would be fine. I'm so glad you two decided to sign on to our little project."

"And what project is that?" Miguel repositioned the laptop so Jack didn't have to stretch so far to be in the picture.

"Well, at the moment, I'm not at liberty to go into details but I can say, it is something right up your alley."

"Yeah? And what is that?" Jack asked.

"Preserving endangered species."

"So why are we here? In Tanzania?" Miguel inquired.

"No, let me guess," Jack said, thinking back to their website and the long list of endangered species near extinction in different regions all over the world. "Is it the black rhinoceros?"

"No," Nora replied. "You are there to find a mngwa."

Miguel let out a laugh. "You can't be serious. They don't exist."

"I have good reason to believe they do."

Jack was skeptic. He'd heard stories about the giant black leopard supposedly as tall as a zebra. Swahili fairy tales meant to frighten children.

"I trust you inspected the tranquilizer guns provided?"

"Yes, we've used these types before." Jack knew the air rifles were equipped with .50 caliber darts meant for big game.

"Each syringe is filled with Etorphine, the same opioid used to immobilize elephants," Nora said. "That should be enough to paralyze the animal and give you ample time to get me a blood sample."

"Sounds more like a job for the Red Cross," Miguel said with a smirk.

"Sure you don't want us to video tape it or get some cute pictures?" Jack grinned, trying not to laugh.

"If you two don't feel you are up to the task..."

"No, no, I'm sorry," Jack said, sensing they had crossed the line. "We have this covered."

"Very well, then. Your pilot will remain there until you are done."

Jack glanced out the passenger window. The sky on the horizon was already turning a purplish-pink. He looked back at the computer screen. "It's almost dusk."

"I know."

"And you want us traipsing around in the dark looking for this thing?"

"What better time? Remember, the mngwa is a nocturnal hunter."

"You really think we're going find one, just like that?"

"Yes, I do. Good luck." Nora's image disappeared as the screen went black.

"This is nuts," Jack said.

"I'll say. But as long as they're willing to pay us the big bucks, who are we to argue?" Miguel closed up his laptop. He called to the pilot. "We're through talking with the professor."

The pilot stepped from the cockpit. He went down the narrow aisle to the side hatch. He released the locking mechanism, pushed the door out and up, extending the bottom step of the stairs down to the ground.

The outside heat blasted through the opening.

"You might want to hurry it up." The pilot wiped his brow.

Jack buckled his gun belt. He took out his revolver. He flipped open the cylinder to make sure there were six cartridges. He snapped it shut, sliding the barrel back in the holster.

Miguel slipped on his shoulder rig. He ejected the clip from the Desert Eagle to make sure it was full then slapped it back into the handle.

They opened the two black cases, removing the tranquilizer guns, making sure to bring along the plastic box of darts. Each rifle had a gun-mounted 170 lumens spotlight on the underside of the barrel, eliminating the need for flashlights.

Miguel went out first, stepping down to the dirt. Jack turned to the pilot before going down the stairs. "I guess you're waiting here?"

The pilot sat in a passenger seat, brandishing a military-style assault rifle. "Someone's got to watch the plane."

***

Rather than go directly into the village, Jack and Miguel took a short hike along the base of the foothill while there was still light. If there was a predator, it would most likely come down from higher ground. They conducted a search even though they didn't expect to find anything. There were no giant paw prints or large piles of scat or any evidence suggesting that a big cat had been prowling around the vicinity.

"How's your Swahili?" Jack asked Miguel as they crossed the clearing and approached the village made up of a dozen, round, mud-walled huts with rough-edge thatched roofs that looked like bad haircuts. In the center of the huts was a small pen of goats.

"Better than your Spanish."

"See if I ever order you a margarita again." Jack counted maybe twenty-five people clustered together in front of one of the huts. The village men were dressed in cast-me-down clothes: soiled T-shirts with famous brand names on the front, dirt-stained trousers, and sandals; the boys with similar-style shirts but wearing shorts. The women and the girls wore white headscarves, brightly colored cloaks, and white caftans.

A tall man with a thick black beard—and bright red Coca-Cola T-shirt— stood at the front of the group: obviously the leader. Jack doubted if the man would be considered a chief or a shaman.

Miguel handed his tranquilizer gun to Jack. He walked over to the leader of the village. Jack watched Miguel struggle through an introduction, gesturing with his hands, and pausing to think of the correct words in Swahili. At first the village leader seemed confused. After a few exchanges, the man understood what Miguel was trying to convey. They quickly cut through the communication barrier.

The sun disappeared behind the hills. Nightfall crept over the village.

Two men piled some wood, lighting a small bonfire near the huts away from the goats. The flames cast their shadows on the curved adobe walls.

Miguel shook the tribal leader's hand. He walked back over to Jack.

"So what did he say when you told him why we're here?" Jack handed Miguel back his dart gun.

"He hopes we catch the evil spirit."

"You mean he actually believes there's a mngwa?"

"The villagers call it Nunda, Eater of People."

"And they've seen it?"

"Not really. He said it comes in the night sometimes and steals their goats."

"That could be anything. A hyena or a lion."

"He said one of the goat herders went out searching for a stray but never came back."

"And you believe that?"

"I don't know."

"So if he's telling the truth, we're talking about some kind of man-eater?" Even though Jack was dead set against putting down any animal, he knew when to draw the line, especially when it came to confronting a dangerous killer such as a rogue lion. "Nora never mentioned anything about a villager getting killed."

"Maybe she didn't know."

Jack glanced down at his tranquillizer rifle. "Suddenly, this doesn't seem like much of a weapon."

The only source of light came from the bonfire. The villagers were gathered around the flames, but not for its warmth. The fire was meant to scare off marauding predators.

For two hours, Jack and Miguel paced the perimeter of the village.

When it reached the third hour, they were tired even though they were supposed to be on high alert. Every crackle of the fire sounded like a snapping twig out in the surrounding darkness.

All but a few villagers had retired to their huts. Soon, they too, went to their homes.

"What time do you have?" Miguel asked Jack.

Jack illuminated the blue dial on his wristwatch. "Just after eleven."

"What do you want to do? Everyone's gone to sleep."

"Think there's any coffee on the plane?"

"We're giving up?"

"No."

"I guess it wouldn't hurt to go see. I'd like to use the restroom onboard, splash some water on my face."

"Which way is it?" Jack turned and looked around.

"The plane's over there." Miguel pointed at the lights shining out of the oval-shaped cabin windows, half the distance of a football field away.

"As soon as we've recharged, we'll come back." Jack tucked his dart rifle under his arm, aiming the beam of light directly in front of him.

Except for the lights on their guns and those from the plane, the night around them was pitch black.

Jack couldn't recall if there was a moon or if it was obscured behind the dark clouds blocking the stars.

A menacing growl sounded behind them.

"Did you hear that?" Jack spun around. He shined his light into the darkness but saw nothing.

"What the hell was that?"

The growl came from a different direction.

"Damn, whatever that is, it sure is fast. I didn't even hear it move," Miguel gasped.

"Or there's two of them."

"No, that sounded like the same growl."

Jack got an eerie feeling. He turned to Miguel "Ever see the movie *American Werewolf in London*?"

"Years ago."

"Remember the scene in the beginning when the two guys are walking through the moors in the middle of the night?"

"You mean beware of the moon and stay on the path?"

"Yeah. Doesn't this kind of remind you of that?" Jack said.

Miguel shined his light about but the beam was too weak to see very far.

"We better keep going." Jack picked up the pace, afraid if they started running it'd only make them look like easy prey. He glanced over his shoulder. He saw a huge shape loping after them. "Shit, it's coming. Run!"

The men dashed across the dirt field, their lights bobbing up and down.

Jack shined his light directly into the window where the pilot was sitting, reading a magazine. "Hey! Hey! Open the damn door!"

The pilot squinted through the window. He opened the hatch, lowering the stairs to the ground.

Jack heard footfalls closing so he aimed the muzzle of the tranquillizer gun over his shoulder. He fired blindly, hoping for a lucky shot.

The giant panther came to an abrupt halt at the edge of the light shining down on the ground from the open hatchway. It was five feet tall at the shoulders. Jack figured it had to weigh four hundred pounds.

The dart was sticking out of its chest.

"Shouldn't it be hitting the ground by now?" Jack stepped back toward the stairs. Miguel was nearly to the bottom step.

The mngwa dipped its head, lowering into a crouch preparing to pounce.

"Get down!" the pilot yelled standing in the open doorway. The muzzle flash of his assault rifle lit up the night. A long burst of bullets zinged over Jack and Miguel's heads. Spent shells littered the passenger compartment floor. The pilot quickly ran out of bullets. "Get on the plane and close the hatch," he yelled, dashing for the cockpit.

Jack figured the mngwa was dead for sure. He looked at the spot where it had been standing. The big cat was gone. It had disappeared into thin air like a ghost.

The plane's twin engines started revolving the propellers.

Miguel was halfway up the stairs when the plane started moving. "Jesus, he's taking off and we haven't even pulled up the stairs."

The mngwa leaped out of the blackness, landing on the stairs as Jack and Miguel dove onto the floor of the passenger compartment. The giant panther clung to the side of the plane, its sharp talons piercing the thin metal. It stuck its head inside, roaring at the two men.

The Cessna ascended, its left wing dipping drastically due to the added weight of the mngwa, causing Jack and Miguel to cling to the seats or slide into the deadly jaws of the big cat. The engines sputtered. The aircraft was losing power...

The mngwa's mouth went slack. Its head drooped on its chest.

"We're going to crash!" Miguel yelled.

"Help me push it off!"

The two men placed their boots on the big cat's chest. It took all of their strength to dislodge the animal's curved claws. Jack yanked the dart out of the mngwa's chest as it fell away, disappearing into the night sky.

The pilot righted the plane. "Close the damn hatch!"

Miguel got down on the floor. He pulled up the stairs while Jack reached up and brought down the upper part of the hatch. Once the door was closed, Jack drew down the lever bar. "Jesus, did that just happen?" He collapsed in a seat.

"Won't be terrorizing that village anymore." Miguel sat down beside Jack.

"Yeah, but if there's one, there has to be more."

"Just be thankful she didn't expect us to capture the thing alive."

Jack showed Miguel the dart with blood smeared on the needle. "She did say all she wanted was a blood sample, right?"

Miguel grinned. "Then I'd say, mission accomplished."

17

BURU

Instead of returning to the Hawe Wildlife Preserve, the pilot flew to Dar es Salaam, landing at Julius Nyerere International Airport. A man in a black polo shirt with a WE emblem above the pocket was waiting for Jack and Miguel. He introduced himself simply as David. He was instructed to retrieve the blood sample for Professor Howard.

Jack handed David the bagged dart with the mgnwa's dried blood.

"Are either of you carrying firearms?"

"In our bags," Jack said.

"Then you'll need to give them to me so I can clear airport security."

Jack and Miguel dug through their duffel bags. They relinquished their gun belts and weapons. David put them inside a small green travel bag he'd brought with him.

"A shower and a good night's sleep would be nice," Jack said.

"Already arranged."

Jack and Miguel followed David to a security door, which he opened with a swipe of a card. They went up a flight of stairs and through another door taking them into the main terminal.

"Before I take you to your hotel, I suggest we pick up your tickets so tomorrow you'll have your boarding passes. I've already cleared you with customs and the TSA."

"Sounds good," Jack said.

"This guy sure knows his way around," Miguel whispered to Jack.

David walked up to a KLM check-in counter. He exchanged greetings with the ticket agent, a striking African woman. She gave David a big smile like they were accustomed to doing business with each other. David placed the travel bag on a platform next to the agent's counter.

The agent bent down, affixing identification and airline tags to the luggage handle. She placed the bag on a moving conveyor belt taking it through two large plastic flaps in the wall where it disappeared.

The woman handed Jack and Miguel their tickets.

Jack noted the destination. "Dukuh International Airport. Where's that?"

"Jakarta. In Indonesia."

"My God," Miguel said. "That's got to be, what, five-thousand miles?"

"A ten-hour flight," the agent said.

"Come, I have a car waiting to take us to your hotel." David moved away from the counter, motioning for Jack and Miguel to follow him. "You'll need to get plenty of rest. Your plane leaves tomorrow at ten a.m. sharp."

Jack sighed as Miguel let out a groan.

***

The next day proved to be hellishly longer than they anticipated, even after enduring the 10-hour flight to Jakarta and the advanced four-hour time difference because they had to change airlines and catch a chartered flight on Aviastar for the rest of the 1,100-mile leg of the trip to Namrole Airport on the island of Buru.

An hour before they landed, Miguel received a notification on ChatLine from Nora on his laptop.

Again, the professor was sitting behind her desk. This time she had an apologetic look on her face. "I want to thank you both for getting me the mgnwa blood sample."

"You already have it?" Jack said surprisingly, leaning in so Nora could see him.

"Oh, yes. I understand it was rather a horrifying experience."

"You might say that," Miguel said.

"Thank God neither of you were hurt."

"Just doing our jobs," Jack said.

"So, what are we after this time?" Miguel asked, getting down to business.

Nora showed them an illustration of a giant prehistoric-looking lizard. "This is an artist's rendition of a Buru."

"Looks like a Komodo dragon," Jack said.

"Yes, but the Buru is much larger."

"How large?" Miguel asked.

"They're believed to be over fifteen feet long."

"You said *believed.* It this another one of your cryptids?"

"That's right. When you land, I've arranged for a guide to meet you at the airport. And I must warn you, if the Buru is anything like the Komodo..."

"I know, don't stick our heads in their mouths?" Jack joked.

"Not funny, Jack. One bite and their saliva will cause your flesh to rot."

"Jesus."

"Good luck, and please, be careful." Nora faded to black, ending the chat.

***

Where the Tanzania savanna had been arid and intolerably hot, the climate on Buru was sweltering and insufferably humid as they stepped from the plane down the truck-mounted passenger stairs onto the shimmering tarmac.

Jack and Miguel went inside to baggage claim where their duffle bags and the green travel bag containing their guns were waiting on a luggage turnstile.

An Indonesian man with a shaved head was waiting for them at the curbside pickup area. He wore a black tank top to display his heritage tattoos covering both arms and his upper chest. He stood next to a battered high-suspension Toyota truck with a rusted roll bar behind the cab. Oversized tires extended out of the wheel wells.

"Hello. I am Panut. Your guide."

"Hi, there," Jack replied.

"Did you say Peanut?" Miguel asked.

"Panut," the man corrected.

Miguel smiled. "Sorry. Must be the jet lag."

Jack wiped his forehead with his shirtsleeve, giving the man's truck the once-over. "You have air in that?"

"Oh, yeah. Plenty air."

"Thank goodness for that."

Jack and Miguel threw their duffle bags into the bed of the truck. Panut looked at the green travel bag in Jack's hand.

"Dat go in back."

"It's our guns," Jack said. "I'd rather keep them in the cab."

"No room. Put in back."

Jack tried to hide his annoyance. He glanced inside the truck. The cab was so small he seriously doubted if all three of them would even fit. He certainly wasn't going to ride in the back of the truck in this heat.

"All right. I see your point." Jack wedged the travel bag between the two duffle bags in front of the spare tire, some yard tools, a bunch of crinkled beer cans, two metal poles, and a coil of clothesline.

Jack opened the passenger door. He looked at Miguel. "Age before beauty."

"Shut up. I'm younger than you."

"Just get in."

Miguel climbed inside. He slid halfway across the bench seat, both knees pressed up against the bottom of the dashboard.

Jack got in. He was just able to close the door.

Panut got behind the steering wheel. He started up the truck, which rattled and vibrated as though every bolt holding it together was ready to fall out. Being a smaller man, he had plenty of room where Jack and Miguel were like two left feet stuffed in a single sock.

The driver and passenger windows were rolled all the way down.

They headed away from the airport onto a major roadway. Jack was feeling sticky from the humid air rushing in. He saw only a car radio on the dashboard that looked like it had been taken from another vehicle, possibly stolen, and jury-rigged to fit.

Jack looked across Miguel at Panut. "I thought you said this had air-conditioning?"

"This is air," Panut said, waving his free hand at the opened windows.

Miguel broke out laughing.

"Swell." Jack sat back against the vinyl seat.

Panut turned off the main roadway. He sped down a narrow dirt road into the jungle.

Jack grabbed the top of the window frame so he wouldn't crush Miguel when they came around a bend.

For forty minutes, the truck barreled down the same road.

Thundering up a grade, Jack leaned his head out. He glanced down at the steep drop off of sheer rock. "How much further?" he yelled to Panut.

"Not far!" Panut hollered back, reaching a summit only to speed down the winding road.

Jack could feel every spring in the seatback stabbing into his spine. He was definitely going to need a few therapeutic sessions with a good chiropractor after this trip.

Up ahead, the dirt road ended abruptly. Panut didn't slow down. He kept driving straight into the jungle.

"Hey, what are you doing?" Miguel's hands shot up to the headliner to brace against the jolting ride; large fronds slapping the windshield; the front bumper grill guard plowing down brush and high grass.

Just when Jack thought they were going to slam into a tree, Panut cut the wheel. The truck burst out of the dense vegetation, rolling to a stop in a small clearing near a marshland surrounded by tropical trees.

Panut shut off the engine. He looked at Jack and Miguel. "See, not far."

They climbed out of the truck.

Panut jumped up into the truck bed.

Jack leaned over the side of the rear fender. "So what did you bring us?"

The Indonesian guide picked up two long spears.

"What, no tranquillizer guns?" Miguel said.

"Skin too tough. Spears work better. See?" Panut twisted the spearhead off a pole. "Hollow tip. Trap blood inside."

Jack looked at the six-foot long poles in Panut's hands. "You really think we can get close enough to actually jab one of these things?"

"Jack, we have to find one first," Miguel said. "Personally, I don't think these things are real."

"Well, whatever is out there, I'm not going in with just a pig sticker." Jack reached over, grabbing the green travel bag from the truck bed. He opened the bag. He took out his revolver, strapping on his gun belt. Miguel put on his shoulder rig. They took a moment to load their weapons.

Once they were ready, Panut pointed the way. Jack and Miguel carried their spears. They followed the guide across the clearing into the marsh grass.

Jack got a whiff of something foul up ahead. "What is that smell?"

"Getting close," Panut said.

Miguel covered his nose with his hand. "Man, that stinks."

Jack could hear a humming getting steadily louder with each step.

They stumbled onto a spot where the grass had been flattened in a large circle fifteen feet across, filled with rotting carcasses swarming with black flies. Some of the skeletal remains were still intact. Jack recognized a wild boar and a few deer.

Miguel held a handkerchief over his mouth and nose. He studied a pile of bones. "Jack, take a look at this."

Jack stared down at the ground. "That's definitely a human skull. Looks like we're not the first to come here?" He looked at their guide.

Panut shook his head.

"So what is this place?"

"Buru feed here. From here, watch your step."

They continued to hike into the eight-foot tall grass. The blades were sharp as razors, slicing at their hands and faces. The stalks so resilient, they'd pop right back up after being trampled flat to the ground. They soon lost sight of one another, like being separated in a cornfield maze.

Miguel yelled for help.

18

QUAGMIRE

"Jesus, what did you do?" Jack said, once he cleared the tall grass and saw Miguel standing waist-deep in the middle of a swampy pond.

Panut came running over to join Jack on the bank.

"Stay calm," Jack told Miguel.

"Easy for you to say. You're not the one standing in the middle of quicksand."

"I told you. Watch your step," Panut said.

"Thanks, Panut. Next time I'll be more careful," Miguel said sarcastically.

"Try and not to move around," Jack instructed. "The more you do, the faster you'll sink. Where's your pole?"

"I dropped it when I fell in. It's gone."

"Okay, then grab mine." Jack extended his pole. Miguel attempted to turn around to grab the end but it was just out of reach. The slightest movement caused him to slip down another inch into the oatmeal mush.

"I can't," Miguel said.

"Okay, forget that. Try lying back. See if you can raise your feet."

Miguel put his arms out to the side. He lowered his head back, hoping to float.

"Don't panic. We'll figure this out." Jack searched around for something they could use to throw to Miguel. He remembered seeing the spool of clothesline in the bed of the truck. "Panut, go back and get the rope from your truck."

Panut dashed off through the reeds.

Miguel continued to sink.

"Breathe deep," Jack yelled to his friend. "The more air in your lungs the more buoyant you'll be. Just hold tight. Panut will be back and we'll get you out."

Miguel moved his arms over his head, attempting a slow backstroke.

"That's right. Swim! You can do it," Jack yelled, shouting words of encouragement. "Don't worry, buddy. We'll have you out before..."

Something big rushed through the high grass.

Jack heard a hiss like a ruptured gas line.

"Shit, what the hell was that?" Miguel said, finally able to turn enough he could see Jack. His eyes widened. "Jack! Watch out!"

Jack spun around with his spear pointed directly in front of him.

A gigantic lizard stepped out of the tall grass onto the bank. The enormous head and body were covered with scaly skin like linked metal rings of chainmail worn by medieval knights. It had extremely long curled claws causing it to walk awkwardly. With each step, its fork-tipped tongue shot out of its mouth, sucking back in like a paper party horn.

Nora had been right. The Buru was easily fifteen feet long from its snout to the tip of its long powerful tail. It had to weigh close to five hundred pounds. If it was anything like its cousin, the Komodo dragon, it was probably fast on its feet.

As it approached Jack, the Buru opened its mouth wide like a massive hissing snake exposing its pink-gums and fanged teeth.

A man's hand was partially visible down its gullet.

Panut stumbled out of the reeds. His face was pale. The stump at the end of his arm looked like it had been dipped in red paint.

At first, Jack thought the man looked ashen from the blood loss: the front of his tank top and pants drenched. But then he realized it was much more serious than merely bleeding to death. The skin on Panut's face and arms was sloughing off like boiled meat falling off the bone.

He was literally rotting in front of Jack. The man had turned into a walking zombie, all due to the Buru's deadly saliva.

It was heartbreaking to see the man dying right in front of him but then there was a breath of hope—for Miguel—as Panut had been able to retrieve the clothesline that had come uncoiled and was dragging behind him.

Panut staggered to the edge of the bank. He fell facedown into the quicksand like a lead weight. He steadily sank into the quagmire, dragging the clothesline down with him.

The Buru decided at that moment to lunge.

Jack jabbed it in the chest with his spear.

Only when he pulled back to stab the creature again, he found the spearhead had lodged in the thick hide. The giant lizard stepped back, yanking the spear from Jack's hands.

He stood dazed for a second.

Time enough for the Buru to repeat its attack and for Miguel to drag his Desert Eagle out of his shoulder holster and fire off a well-aimed high-caliber shot. The bullet struck the creature in the shoulder, punching a decent-sized hole in the lizard's seemingly impenetrable armored skin.

The Buru roared. It spun around, stepping on the shaft, pulling the spearhead out before bolting back into the tall grass.

"Jack! The rope!" Miguel yelled.

Jack dove to the ground like he was a baseball player sliding headfirst into second base. He grabbed the end of the rope before it went under with Panut. He pulled as much rope up as he needed and cut the line.

He formed a lasso, throwing the lifeline to his friend. Miguel slipped the noose over his head and shoulder. Jack pulled on the rope; hand over hand, until Miguel was on the bank.

"Thanks. I owe you a beer," Miguel said. He was covered with wet clinging sand from the shoulders down.

"I wish I could have done something for Panut."

"Do you think the professor realizes the danger involved?"

"I'm starting to wonder. For all we know, those bones back in that pit belong to some poor schmuck she sent before us."

"That's not a comforting thought." Miguel looked over at the blood smeared on the spearhead lying on the bank. "Well, at least we got her damn blood sample."

"Yeah, but it's certainly not worth a man's life."

"I really have to get out of these clothes," Miguel said. "Feels like the time Maria and I took mud baths in Calistoga."

"Too bad you don't have a hose to spray out those nooks and crannies," Jack smirked, picking up the spear.

"I doubt you'd be laughing with sand up your crack." Miguel grabbed his waistband, shook his trousers then stumped his boots to shake out the wet grit.

Jack unscrewed the spearhead and threw the pole down. He drew his revolver and cocked back the hammer. "Let's get out of here before that thing decides to come back."

This time on their way back through the tall grass they kept together, never letting the other one out of his sight.

The smell—now that they knew what it was—seemed twice as bad as they skirted the perimeter of the Buru's abattoir.

Jack was never so glad to see Panut's truck when they finally reached the clearing.

Miguel already had his shirt off. He ran up to the side of the truck, slipped off his boots, and stripped out of his pants. He grabbed a jug of water from inside the cab, dousing his head to wash off. Without bothering to dry himself, he dug out a change of clothes from his bag. He quickly got dressed while Jack kept watch.

Jack opened the driver's door. He climbed behind the steering wheel while Miguel got in the passenger side.

"Oh, shit. Jack!" Miguel pointed through the windshield. The monstrous lizard was charging straight at the truck.

Jack reached for the steering column...

There was no starter key in the ignition switch.

"Where's the key?" Jack shot a look at Miguel. "Please don't tell me Panut has it on him."

"Try under the mat," Miguel said in a panic. He placed his arm over the side mirror bracket trying to line up a shot.

The Buru moved to the other side of the truck.

Jack bent over. He pulled up the floor mat. "No, not under here."

"Here it comes!" Miguel yelled.

Jack glanced out the open driver's window.

The Buru did a belly run at the truck, ramming the fender and driver's door.

As his window was open, Jack was afraid the lizard would stick its head inside the cab.

One bite and that would be it.

Jack reached down for his revolver on the seat.

The Buru struck the side of the truck again, this time lifting the tires on the driver's side off the ground. Jack held onto the steering wheel as the cab tilted.

"If that thing flips us over, we're dead," Miguel said.

Jack reached for his gun but it slid off, falling beneath the seat.

Miguel pointed his .357 pistol at Jack.

"What are you doing?" Jack shouted in disbelief.

"Don't move!" Miguel fired two shots into the door panel, narrowly missing the top of Jack's thighs. The high-caliber bullets tore twin holes above the armrest.

The Buru roared. The truck slammed to the ground.

A key attached to a bottle opener fell down from the visor, dropping into the palm of Jack's hand. "Well, I'll be damned." He inserted the key. He turned the ignition switch. The starter motor groaned like the battery was dying.

"Oh, don't tell me..." Jack tried it again. The engine fired up.

"Drive! Drive!" Miguel yelled.

Jack threw the truck into gear, stomping on the gas.

They drove back through the jungle, never once looking back.

19

AHOOL

As soon as they were back on the dirt road, Jack pulled over so Miguel could get out to retrieve his laptop from his bag in the bed of the truck.

Miguel sent a quick email message to Nora explaining what happened and that Panut was dead. Not knowing how to proceed, they decided to wait.

Ten minutes later they got a response.

Miguel took a moment to read the reply.

"What does she say?" Jack asked.

"It's not from her. It's Ivan Connors, head of security of Wilde Enterprises."

"How did he get involved?"

"I don't know. Maybe he's monitoring employee emails."

"Sounds like big brother's watching the professor. So, what's up?"

"He wants us to take the truck to a designated lot at the airport and leave it. We're not to say anything to anyone. We're to go to the main terminal and wait for further instructions."

"Shouldn't we be telling the authorities? A wild animal killed Panut. Well, technically you could say he died in the quicksand but still somebody should do something. Surely, his family would want his body found."

"Connors said it's a company matter now and he'll handle it."

"Sounds like a cover-up to me."

"Be happy we're off the hook."

"Just doesn't feel right." Jack started up the truck while Miguel signed off his email account to plot a GPS course back to the airport.

***

Everything seemed to be operating like a well-oiled machine. As soon as Jack and Miguel stepped into the terminal, they heard a page on the intercom requesting they report to the Aviastar ticket counter where they were handed two tickets for Java.

Miguel let out a grumbling laugh. “What are we, a couple of ping pong balls?”

“Why, what’s so funny?” Jack threw his duffle bag over his shoulder as they walked to the waiting area to make their connection.

“First we’re at Jakarta and fly over a thousand miles to get here. And now we’re getting on a plane and flying to Java which is only a couple hundred miles from where we started.”

“Hey, at least we’re racking up frequent flier miles.” Jack looked down at his wristwatch. “Hey, we better get a move on, our flight’s just about to leave.”

***

Somewhere over the Flores Sea, Professor Howard contacted Miguel on his laptop. This time she insisted they use earphones, as she didn’t want any passengers to overhear her part of the conversation. Miguel plugged in a splitter cable so Jack could listen in.

“I was so sorry to hear about Panut.” This time Nora was not at her desk but sitting in a padded armchair. Her eyes were bloodshot.

“You knew him personally?” Jack couldn’t tell if she’d been crying or was exhausted from working long hours.

“We met when I was in Buru.”

“So you’ve *actually* been there?” Miguel asked.

“You know, I do step out of the laboratory on occasion.”

“So you knew the dangers?” Jack said.

“I did. And I should have prepared you. I’m sorry.” Nora rubbed her right eye.

Jack saw a tear trickle down her cheek.

“So this place we’re going to now. What can we expect?” Miguel asked.

“When you land, you’ll find a truck rental waiting. I’ll send you the coordinates to where a guide will be waiting for you.”

“And what will we be looking for exactly?” Jack asked.

“Indonesian short-nose fruit bats. *Pteropus.* They’re a species of megabat. Find them and it should lead you to our real prize. The ahool.”

“Is that like the flying fox?” Jack asked, thinking back to the endangered species list posted on their blog.

“If you’re referring to the giant golden-crown flying fox, those are in the Philippines and have been reported as weighing three pounds with a wingspan of six feet. No, the ahool is much, much bigger.”

“How big?” Miguel had to ask.

"Hopefully, next time we talk, you'll be telling me."

"I've got a question," Jack asked.

"What's that?"

"Why only blood and not try and capture these creatures."

"Are you volunteering?"

"Not exactly."

"It's safer this way," Nora assured.

"But what do you do with the blood?"

"All part of our research. I better sign off. And please, do be careful."

The computer screen went to black.

"You don't think this is a little bit strange?" Jack asked Miguel. "Why all the secrecy about what they do with the blood?"

"It's quite obvious." Miguel closed his laptop.

"Yeah? Care to share?"

"She's a vampire."

"Real funny," Jack said, but he wasn't laughing.

***

After landing and getting their rental vehicle—a four-wheel drive Ford Explorer with a moldy-smelling interior—Miguel plotted a GPS route taking them to a disused logging road snaking deep into the jungle. When they arrived at their destination, a barefoot man wearing a black songkok cap, gray over-sized shirt, and a sarong was waiting for them, sitting on a log.

Jack and Miguel got out of the Explorer to introduce themselves.

"I am Teguh." The guide gave them a bow.

Jack noticed a large tooth hanging on the end of a chain around Teguh's neck. "Is that from a jaguar?"

Teguh rubbed his thumb over the smooth surface of the fang. "Ahool."

"No way that's a bat tooth. That has to be over three inches long," Miguel said.

"So how do we snare one of these things?" Jack looked around. He didn't see any tranquilizer guns to subdue the animal or spears with the ability to collect blood samples.

Teguh picked up his rifle leaning against the log.

"Now there's a relic." Jack recognized the World War II vintage M1 Garand.

"We hunt." Teguh raised the .30 caliber rifle in the air like a Native American Indian on horseback ready to charge into battle.

"Wait a minute," Miguel said. "We're not here to kill it. We just need some of its blood."

"I get you blood." Teguh took off down a narrow trail into the tropical forest.

Jack looked at Miguel. "Do you think he understood?"

"I don't know. But we better not lose him." Miguel headed down the path.

Jack followed closely behind.

Teguh kept to a steady pace as they hiked through the trees, the thick canopy blocking out the sky.

Jack felt something squish under his boot. He looked down. He'd stepped on a half-rotten piece of fruit. The ground around him was littered with ripened fruit having fallen from the trees.

"We're in the middle of a mango grove," Miguel said.

Teguh stood close to a tree trunk. He threw back the bolt action on the M1 Garand. He stared up into the overhead branches.

"What is it?" Jack asked.

"They're up there."

"What?" Jack put his hand on the grip of his Colt revolver. He gazed up at an opening between the treetops. He shielded his eyes from the sun. "All I see are mangoes."

"Those aren't mangoes," Miguel said. "They're bats!"

"Jesus, they're huge."

Teguh fired off a single shot into the air.

Hundreds of screeching bats burst from the branches.

The startled creatures descended on them like a screeching twister.

Jack covered his head, dropping to his knees. The frantic bats swirled around him, their clawed feet raking the back of his shirt.

A bat crashed to the ground. It had a wingspan of four feet. It looked like a three-pound rodent strapped to a hand glider. Still stunned from the fall, the bat used its claws on the front of its wings to pull itself across the ground toward a nearby bush.

A giant winged beast crashed through the trees with a deafening shriek, scattering the fruit bats.

Jack could feel the powerful wings buffeting the air around him; swirling dust like rotary blades of a hovering helicopter. He glanced up at the colossal megabat looking as though it had flown off the page of a graphic horror novel. The bat's wings were as broad as a skydiver's parachute. It had massive four-talon feet big enough to snatch up a large sheep.

The ahool swooped down, sinking its claws into Teguh's shoulders. Teguh screamed. He dropped his rifle. The giant bat hoisted the man into the air, as he kept kicking his bare feet all the way up into the treetops.

Miguel stood, brushing some guano off his shirt. "How are we going to explain this one? That makes two guides now we've lost."

"Definitely not good." Jack saw the M1 Garand lying on the ground. He walked over, picking up the rifle. He noticed Teguh's necklace in the dirt. He snatched up the chain, putting it in his shirt pocket.

Miguel did a slow pivot while staring down the gun sight of his Desert Eagle. "I don't think I want to be around when that thing comes back."

"I'm with you brother."

They hustled back along the trail to where they had parked the Explorer.

Miguel sat in the front passenger seat. He immediately turned on his laptop.

After a few minutes, they had Nora on ChatLine. She looked apprehensive, as though she wasn't expecting them to contact her so soon indicating something had gone wrong.

Miguel relayed what had happened. That Teguh was probably dead, though there was no real way of confirming unless they went back which they had no intention of doing.

She reacted to the terrible news by saying, "Oh my God. Does this mean you weren't able to get a blood sample?"

"Whoa. A man just died. I mean, we think he did." Jack couldn't believe her callousness.

"I'm sorry, I really am. I know how insensitive that must have sounded but I've been under a lot of pressure."

"Maybe it's time you explained what we're *really* doing out here."

"I will, Jack, but not just yet. I really wish you could have gotten me something from the ahool."

"Wait a minute." Jack took Teguh's necklace out of his shirt pocket.

"What do you have there?" Nora leaned closer to the camera lens on the top of her computer, making her face appear bigger on Miguel's screen.

Jack held up the chain. "Teguh was wearing it. He said the tooth was from an ahool."

"Oh my God, Jack. That's fantastic news!"

"It is?"

"Go back to the airport. We'll arrange to have someone meet you there and get the tooth."

"And then what?"

"You'll be given your next assignment."

Jack and Miguel watched the laptop screen go blank.

"I don't know about you, Jack, but I think I'm ready for a little vacation from all this."

"You and me, both."

20

SOCOTRA

Located off the horn of Somalia near the Gulf of Arden and the Arabian Sea, the island of Socotra had been described as "the most alien-looking place on Earth."

As a kid, Jack and his parents spent many weekends and vacations traveling to different states, camping and hiking. Many of his favorite places were memorable because of their strange landscapes like watching the dead moonscape of the limestone pinnacles in Mono Lake, California, transform into a fantasy world during a purplish sunset or witnessing the active hydrothermal geysers in Yellowstone National Park, Wyoming, spewing like clockwork every minutes or trekking the floor of Bryce Canyon, Utah, and gawking up at the 10-story rock spires.

As wondrous as those locations were to him growing up, he had to admit the archipelago island was the most bizarre with its unusual rocky topography and plant life; dragon blood trees that looked like giant green umbrellas and behemoth cucumber trees that sprouted right out of the rocks like gigantic sweet potatoes crowned with budding flowers making the land appear like a magical kingdom.

The isolated island was only eighty miles long and thirty miles wide but was teeming with 700 endemic species of which 37% of the plants were found exclusively on Socotra.

Professor Nora Howard strongly believed of the animals occupying the island, two of the indigenous creatures were on her cryptozoology list, which was why she agreed to Jack and Miguel's request to go there for a little rest and relaxation as long as they squeezed in a couple of cryptid expeditions.

The best part for Miguel was he was able to use some of the funds they had acquired from the past adventures and purchase plane tickets for Maria and Sophia to fly them to the island.

After a blissful reunion at the airport, Miguel, Maria, and Sophia took a shuttle across the island where they drove by urban dwellings constructed of hewn stone with lavishly whitewash-trimmed windowed façades, apartment structures built on the side of high cliffs, some perched precariously on top of seemingly inaccessible buttes.

A short while later, they arrived at a remote stone house on a grassy ridge overlooking a white sandy beach with a spectacular view of the azure blue Indian Sea.

Jack opened the sliding door on the minivan. "Hey, missed you guys."

Sophia jumped into Jack's waiting arms. He spun her playfully.

"I missed you, too, Uncle Jack," a moniker Jack cherished even though there was no blood relation. Not married, and having no kids of his own, it was a nice privilege to be able to share some of Miguel and Maria's joy.

Maria climbed out of the minivan. She gave Jack an affectionate hug, kissing him on the cheek. "Nice to see that woman hasn't gotten you both killed."

"So, I guess Miguel filled you in."

"Every detail."

"Not to worry." Jack turned to introduce the owners of the house. "Maria, Sophia, I would like you to meet Amin Raab and his lovely wife, Asha."

Amin wore a white lightweight shirt, a pair of loose fitting gray pants, and leather sandals. A janbiya was on his belt, the ceremonial dagger worn by Arabic men.

Asha was beautiful and looked stunning in her floor-length burnt orange dress, accentuating her natural curves.

Amin came up first, placing his hands gently on Maria's shoulders. He made a kissing gesture on each of Maria's cheeks though not actually touching her with his lips, but making tiny smacking sounds. Asha stepped forward and repeated the same greeting.

The couple leaned forward, smiled at Sophia, and together said, "Hello."

"Hello," Sophia replied and smiled back. She raised her right hand and shook Amin then Asha's hand.

"Amin and Asha have been kind enough to let us stay with them during our visit," Jack told Maria.

"Thank you so much," Maria said.

"You are so welcome," Asha replied. "I hope you are hungry. I have prepared lunch." Asha showed Maria and Sophia inside the modest home.

"Let me give you a hand with those bags." Jack lugged out two travel suitcases. Miguel paid and thanked the shuttle driver, who drove off and headed back down the rural road.

As soon as they'd put the bags in one of the rooms made up for the Wallas, everyone assembled around a long wooden dining table with benches and a single chair at each end designated for the head of the house and his wife. Asha had gone all out and set out a wonderful feast with bowls of rice and beans and various other dishes.

"To start, we have maraq. I hope you enjoy it," Asha said. Each serving had been poured in a teacup with a spoon and a lemon wedge on the saucer.

Maria tried her soup. "This is very good. What is it?"

"It is a Yemeni lamb broth."

Some of the table settings had a fork, knife, and spoon laid out for the houseguests. Everyone had their own individual salad plates of tomatoes and cucumbers topped with yogurt.

Asha had simmered two types of stews: matfaiya, which was kingfish chunks in a tomato sauce, and fahsah, a hearty lamb stew. She had recently baked so there were four large plates of malawah, a traditional Yemeni flat bread, enough to go around for everyone.

Afterwards for dessert, Asha brought out a tray of freshly fried qamir, sweet dough treats that looked like triangular-shaped egg rolls.

To drink, Asha, Maria, and Sophia had karak, a milk tea made with evaporated milk and cardamon spices. The men capped their meals off with the Arabic coffee, qahwah.

Jack sat back from the table, patting his full stomach. "That was very good, Asha, thank you."

"You are very welcome, Jack."

After lunch, Maria and Sophia helped Asha clear off the table and carry dishes into the kitchen. Amin took Jack and Miguel outside to a small area set up with chairs overlooking the water. He poured raisin wine for the three of them.

"You have yourself quite the paradise," Miguel said, taking a sip of his wine as he enjoyed the magnificent view of the sea.

"Yes. Asha and I are very happy here."

"Have you always lived on the island?" Jack asked.

"No. We came here ten years ago hoping to escape the unrest."

"You're talking about the Yemeni Revolution?"

"That's right. I fear the sea is not wide enough to keep it from our shores. Already soldiers are here patrolling our airport."

"They are intimidating," Miguel said. "Maria and Sophia were a little nervous getting off the plane and walking through the terminal."

"I'm afraid it will only get worse." Amin drank down his wine. He offered to fill Jack and Miguel's glasses, which his guests graciously declined.

"So what's the plan for the rest of the day?" Miguel asked Jack.

"No plan. Have fun with your family."

Miguel looked at Amin. "Is there a path down to the beach?"

"On the other side of those rocks," Amin said, pointing to some boulders on the grassy ridge.

"I think I'll take Maria and Sophia down for a swim. Care to come along?"

Jack shook his head. "Nah, you guys go ahead. I think I'll take a little snooze. Give me time to digest some of Asha's good cooking." Jack looked over at Amin, patting the man on the shoulder.

Amin raised the bottle of raisin wine.

"Ah, what the heck. We're on vacation." Jack held out his glass.

Miguel went inside the house.

Ten minutes later, he came out with Maria and Sophia. He had changed into a pair of swimming trunks and a T-shirt. Maria and Sophia wore two-piece bathing suits. They carried towels over their shoulders. Miguel swung a small wicker basket at his side filled with a glass bottle of fresh well water and a few snack-size morsels of goat's cheese and bread.

Once beyond the rocks, Miguel led the way down a traversing pebble path to the beach. The sand was so white it looked like fine granules of bleached salt. Once they'd picked a spot, Maria and Sophia laid out their towels. Miguel spread his out, placing the picnic basket on one end. He pulled his T-shirt up over his head, tossing it on the towel. "Last one in is a rotten tamale."

Miguel dashed across the sand. He splashed into the water, diving into the crystal clear ocean. He swam underwater for fifty feet then burst up through the surface.

He shook his shaggy black hair like a dog expelling water from its coat.

Standing up to his waist in the water, he raised his arm and yelled, "You better get your..." but then he saw Maria and Sophia standing apprehensively at the water's edge.

"What's wrong?" he yelled.

Maria pointed over Miguel's shoulder. When he turned, he saw half a dozen dorsal fins knifing through the water in a circling pattern, maybe a hundred feet away.

"Miguel, get out of the water!" Maria shouted.

He glanced at the shore. Sophia jumped up and down, screaming, "Daddy, Daddy! Sharks!"

Miguel turned. The fins were no longer cruising in a circle. They were headed straight for him.

"Damn it, Miguel! Get out of there!"

He could see their sleek backs speeding toward him.

Miguel raised his arms and came down fast, slapping his hands on the water. He repeated the movement wanting his presence to be known. He prayed his actions didn't give Maria a heart attack and worry Sophia too much.

The first dolphin whooshed by his right leg, the displacement of water pushing him out of the way. A second dolphin swam by his other side. Soon the entire pod was doing a merry-go-round, curious of this two-legged creature that had ventured into their playground. Knowing they wouldn't harm him, Miguel dipped his hands into the water so his fingertips could caress each passing dolphin.

A school of shiny fish drew the dolphins away.

Miguel waded back to shore.

"Jesus, Miguel, I thought for sure..." Maria wrapped her arms around him as if he was about to accidentally step back off a cliff.

"I was never in any danger."

"You scared me half to death."

"Come in, the water's great."

"Maybe later. Let's go lie in the sun."

"Okay." Miguel felt bad for upsetting Maria. He followed her over to the towels.

Sophia ran up to him. "Daddy, can I look for shells?"

"Sure."

"But stay away from the water," Maria said sternly. "And don't go far. I want to be able to see you."

"Okay, Mama." Sophia shuffled off in the sand.

Miguel lay back on his towel. He gazed up at Maria. She was keeping a vigilant watch on their daughter. Reaching over, he grabbed Maria by the hand and pulled her down on top of him.

"Hey, how am I supposed to...?"

Miguel gave Maria a long passionate kiss. When their lips finally parted, he said, "She'll be fine. Stop your worrying."

"How can I? I worry about you and Jack everyday. These places you go."

"Jack and I are a good team. We watch out for each other. I missed you." Miguel stared into her dark chocolate eyes.

"I missed you, too." Maria gave him a sly smile. She slipped her hand inside the front of Miguel's trunks.

Sophia screamed from somewhere down the beach.

"Oh my God! My baby!" Maria yanked her hand out of Miguel's trunks. She jumped to her feet. She took off like a sprinter coming out of the blocks, kicking sand in Miguel's face.

"Hey! Wait for me." Miguel brushed the sand out of his eyes. He ran after Maria.

Sophia screamed again, sounding even more petrified.

"Sophia! Mama's coming!" Maria yelled.

Miguel caught up, running beside Maria.

The white sand ended.

They saw Sophia standing in the middle of a patch of dirt at the base of the shrubby hillside.

"Sophia, I told you not to wander off." Maria stopped running.

"Are you all right honey?" Miguel could feel his legs burning from the exertion. He took a second to catch his breath and leaned over with his hands on his knees.

Maria stepped onto the dirt.

"Watch out!" Sophia shouted. "They'll come out and get you!"

"Who will?"

Miguel saw a land crab scamper out of a burrow.

The crustacean had a blue-tinted shell, with six legs and two pinchers, one claw twice the size of the other for catching prey while the smaller one was probably used for picking out meat. Its eyes were on two stalks on the top of its eight-inch wide body.

Instead of walking forwards, the crab skittered sideways. It danced around Sophia, making her scream.

"Honey, it's okay. It's only a crab."

The crab raised its pinchers.

Maria started to rush over. Another crab popped up out of the ground right in front of her. "Get out of my way!" When she went to kick the crab, it retreated back into its hole.

Miguel saw more crabs scurry out of their underground dens. They were popping up everywhere.

"Oh my God, Miguel. What do we do?"

"You get Sophia. Let me deal with them." Miguel spotted a piece of driftwood that had washed ashore. It was shaped like a baseball bat. Perfect for what he had in mind. He picked it up, hefting it in his hand.

Sophia raised her arms.

Maria rushed in, scooping her up.

The small army of land crabs circled, clacking their claws like castanets.

Miguel swung the bat. Each time he came close to nailing a crab, it would retreat into the nearest hole. He kept swinging. For every crab that scampered into a hole, another one popped up like a prairie dog.

Maria ran through the melee, carrying Sophia. Miguel threw the stick at a crab descending back into its tunnel. He started walking backwards. Some of the crabs followed, a warning to stay off their turf.

Maria and Sophia were waiting for him on the sandy beach.

"Daddy, you sure showed those crabs," Sophia said.

"Yeah, I guess I did. That was one crazy game of Whack-A-Mole."

21

ARABHAR

Soon after Miguel, Maria, and Sophia came back from their misadventure on the beach, Nora contacted Jack and Miguel to explain their new assignment coinciding with the reason they were staying with the Raabs. This time the stakes were set a little higher.

She wanted them to capture a live specimen.

The following day, Amin took Jack and Miguel to a remote oasis in his battered Toyota Land Cruiser. It was inconceivable to think such a lush tropical setting could exist on such a desolate island. The picturesque date palms and marshy ferns surrounding the mossy-green bottom laguna made for the perfect travel postcard.

Cascading runoff from a high mountain source skimmed down a smooth granite face into the turquoise pool. It was as though they had stumbled onto a hidden treasure.

Jack took it all in. "This is truly amazing."

"Does anyone on the island come here besides you?" Miguel asked Amin.

"No, they are too afraid. This is a sacred place. Islanders think it is cursed by the arabhar."

"What about tourists? I would think once people saw this oasis on the Internet, it would go viral and they'd be flocking to see it."

"This part of the island is forbidden to tourists."

"So how many of these arabhars do you think there are?" Jack asked.

"I do not know. I have only seen one."

Miguel gazed about the surrounding hills. "So what keeps them here? Why don't they migrate somewhere else?"

"This is their home."

"So why are you helping us if these things are sacred?"

"Asha and I enjoy living our simple life. But there will be a time when we will have to leave Socotra. Professor Howard has offered us a generous sum of money so when the time comes we must flee the island, we will be able to resettle somewhere else."

"I understand."

Amin opened the back of the Land Cruiser. He handed Jack and Miguel dogcatcher poles with snares on the ends. Amin grabbed a reptile cage.

He gave Jack and Miguel a serious look. "Be very careful. The arabhar is extremely poisonous."

Amin led the way. They set out through the copse of date palms.

Jack saw something out of the corner of his eye glide between the tree trunks. He spun around. "Did you see that?"

"Be ready," Amin replied.

An elongated shape swooped down out of the branches straight for Miguel. He saw it coming. He raised the looped end of his pole. The elusive creature veered back behind the trees. Another appeared—or was it the same one—dive-bombing over their heads.

At first Jack thought it was a bat but it was longer than the winged mammal and had flesh tone coloring.

Again, Miguel was attacked except this time he was able to cinch the noose around the snake's head. The serpent struggled to break free, flapping its four wings. Miguel held on tight. The flying snake wrapped its wings around its body like a foreskin.

The serpent hissed in Miguel's face.

Amin opened the lid on the reptile cage. "Shove it inside and release the noose."

Miguel lowered the flailing snake. He released the knot, yanking the end of the pole out; Amin slammed down the lid.

Jack grinned at Miguel. "I can't believe it. We did it. And nobody died."

Amin gave Miguel a curious look.

Miguel only shrugged.

22

BLUE BABOON

An hour after Miguel notified Nora they'd successfully captured an arabhar a Bell 206 JetRanger helicopter arrived. The blue and white whirlybird—the letters WE embossed on the fuselage—landed on its skids in a clearing near the Raab's home. The pilot switched off the engine. Jack and Amin waited for the rotor blades to stop spinning.

Jack headed over to the aircraft. Amin carried the metal reptile cage with tiny air holes on the top.

The pilot opened the side door.

"It's only one crate." Jack helped Amin lift the cage into the aircraft.

The pilot strapped the container to the bulkhead so it wouldn't slide on the floor during the flight. "Anything I should know about the cargo?"

"No one told you what you were picking up?"

"I was given a flight plan, nothing else."

The snake banged about inside its metal confines.

The pilot leaned down to peek through the air holes. He heard a loud hiss and backed away.

"I wouldn't get too close."

"What's in there, a python?"

Jack doubted the pilot knew much about herpetology so he decided to make one up. "It's a Socotra Viper. Deadliest snake on the planet."

The pilot regarded the container with newfound respect.

"One bite you're dead." Jack emphasized by snapping his fingers.

"Thanks for telling me."

"Just thought you should know."

The pilot closed the side door. A minute later, the helicopter was back in the sky flying over the ocean.

Jack glanced up the grassy hillside. He saw three tiny silhouettes coming down a path. Soon he recognized Miguel and Maria. Sophia trailed behind her parents.

He decided to go up the path to meet them halfway.

Miguel and Maria were holding hands, swinging their arms. They joined Jack on a flat ledge overlooking the beach.

"The chopper has come and gone. When you get a chance we should check in with Nora." Jack watched Sophia walking toward them. She was holding something blue, cupped in her hands.

Maria gasped when she saw what it was. "Oh my God, Sophia. Put that down."

"Those stupid cats were going to eat it."

Jack saw half a dozen feral cats sitting on the knoll. The island was crawling with them.

Amin came up the path. "Oh, I see you found a blue baboon."

The tarantula in Sophia's hands had a metallic blue carapace with dark blue legs. It was about six inches long, covered with tiny hairs. It seemed content to be held by Sophia.

Miguel looked at Amin. "Is it poisonous?"

"To tell you the truth, I don't know."

"Maybe you should put it down, Sophia," Miguel urged.

"But Papa."

Maria gave her daughter a stern look. "Sophia, do what your father tells you."

Jack heard the tarantula make a noise like someone running a finger down the teeth of a comb.

Amin took a step toward Sophia. "That sound means you should let it go."

The tarantula was already trying to crawl out of Sophia's hands. She lowered the spider to the ground. It strutted off in a slow walk like it was stretching its legs.

Jack saw a mangy cat slinking through the brush. He picked up a stone. He lobbed the rock at the cat to scare it off with no intention of hitting it.

Everyone watched the blue tarantula enter a burrow. It disappeared underground.

Amin smiled. "I came to tell you Asha has prepared supper."

Everyone followed Amin down to the house.

23

HALAH CAVE

The next day Amin drove Jack and Miguel across the island to explore the caverns in search of another cryptid on Nora's list. Entering Halah Cave with its fifty-foot overhanging stalactites and walking between the towering stalagmites was like venturing into the mouth of a behemoth beast with giant teeth.

Jack stared down the dark, cavernous tunnel. He glanced over at Amin, careful not to shine his headlamp directly into the man's eyes. "How far back does it go?"

"Several hundred meters."

"Shouldn't we have brought spelunking gear?" Miguel shone his light up at the steep limestone walls.

"We will not need it. Not for where we are going." Amin pointed to a side passage where the polished gypsum flooring sloped. He grabbed hold of the jutting rock on the wall on his way down to keep from slipping on the slick stone floor.

The cave was as cold as the inside of a refrigerator. Jack heard a constant drip inside the wet cave.

Amin took them to a large chamber. "We should put on our masks."

Jack reached inside his daypack. He slipped the elastic bands around his ears, covering his nose and chin with a blue surgical mask. He put on a pair of safety goggles. He looked over at Amin and Miguel. They were wearing their goggles and masks.

"We only need a small piece of it," Jack said to Amin, his voice muffled behind the mask.

"I understand." Amin grabbed the hilt of a short sword on his belt.

Miguel put his hand out. "Whoa. We're not here to kill it. Just a sliver will do."

"You do know how dangerous this animal is?"

"Nora briefed us, yes."

"Its poisonous breath can kill you."

"Which is why we're wearing these masks."

Amin directed Jack and Miguel to a large rock. "Underneath is a hole where the creature lives. I sealed it myself to keep it from getting out. No one knows that it is there but me. Remove the rock and I will lure it out."

Jack and Miguel stood on each side of the rock. They bent down, lifting together. The rock weighed over fifty pounds. They placed it gently on the ground, afraid if they dropped it the noise would scare off the animal down in the burrow.

Amin removed a pouch from his belt. He widened the drawstring. He took out a clump of meat the size of a softball wrapped in twine to keep it from falling apart.

Jack lifted his mask to sniff the offering. It smelt putrid. "Jeez, what is that?"

"Dead goat."

Jack pulled a handkerchief out of his back pocket. He blew his nose. He knew if he didn't he wouldn't be able to rid himself of the rank smell of rotten meat once he put his mask back on.

Amin lowered the ball of rancid meat attached to a long string. He panned out twenty feet of line, yanking it like a fisherman jiggling a lure to entice a fish. He looped a bit of line around his forefinger and waited patiently.

The line went taut, cinching around his finger so tight the string cut into the flesh, causing Amin to bleed. "Get ready." He retrieved the line, pulling up the half-eaten chunk of meat onto the rocks.

Seconds later, a reptilian head with pinpricks for eyes and two stubby front legs with four-fingered feet rose out of the hole. Pink circular scales segmented the body as big around as a man's wrist. The tazleworm didn't seem afraid of the men. It looked harmless, not at all aggressive.

Amin drew his sword silently. He leaned over slowly, preparing to slice off a piece of its skin. Even a deep cut wouldn't harm the reptile as it had the ability to rejuvenate missing tissue like a lizard growing back a tail after it was bitten off by a predator.

The tazleworm shot out of the hole, snatching the ball of meat in its mouth. The snake-like creature clambered over the rocks with its two small legs, its six-foot long body propelling it forward.

Amin swung his sword. The blade clanged against the stone, missing the creature. "We mustn't let it get away!" He scrambled after it.

Miguel picked up a rock. He tossed it in front of the fleeing tazleworm.

Startled, the creature slithered back.

Miguel scampered after the creature. He leaped and came down, pinning it with his boot. A two-foot section of the giant worm wrapped around his shin.

"Careful, Miguel," Jack warned. He watched the tazleworm rise like a cobra and open its mouth. Instead of baring venom-dripping fangs, the cryptid released a poisonous mist.

Amin's swift blade swooshed over the tazleworm's head. The creature uncoiled around Miguel's leg. Miguel took his foot off the creature. Amin went to stab the thing with the tip of his sword. It was too elusive and slithered back into its hole.

Jack looked at Amin. "What do we do now? Try again?"

"No. That was our only chance. It won't come out now it knows we are here."

"I hope Nora won't be too disappointed." Miguel waited for Jack to help him put the heavy rock back over the hole.

Jack grabbed his side of the rock and lifted. "Hey, we did our best."

"Somehow, I don't think that's going to cut it."

24

DETWAH LAGOON

Professor Howard had been displeased to hear Miguel and Jack failed to get a sample of the tazleworm. Jack tried to make light of it with a lame joke that the thing had been as slippery as an eel covered in olive oil. Nora's sour expression on Miguel's computer screen showed she didn't find the setback humorous. They even volunteered to stay longer in hopes of accomplishing their objective. She told them she had already arranged another assignment for them.

The next morning Maria insisted they take Sophia to the beach one last time before they went to the airport. As Miguel booked them on an afternoon flight there was plenty of time for some fun in the sun. Maria and Sophia were flying to their home in Rocklin Falls, California. Jack and Miguel had a later plane for their next destination.

Instead of going to the beach by the Raab's house, Amin and Asha wanted to take the Walla family and Jack to their favorite spot on the island: Detwah Lagoon.

They traveled in the Land Cruiser. Amin parked on top of the rocky slope so everyone could take in the magnificent view before venturing down to the white sandy beach. As it was low tide they could see the coral shoals just beneath the surface of the shallow turquoise waters. Shorebirds swooped over the outer sandbar stretching out to the navy blue ocean.

Besides swimwear, everyone wore sandals to protect their feet from the rough terrain and hot sand. Once on the beach, they walked down the shoreline toward the edge of the water.

"This is a good spot." Amin laid a blanket on the sand.

Asha kicked off her sandals. She opened a cloth bag. She took out a clear plastic bag filled with six-inch long sardines. "Maria, shall we go for a swim?"

"What are the fish for?"

"For my little pets."

Maria turned to Miguel. "Coming?"

"You two go. I'll keep an eye on Sophia."

Sophia looked up at her father. "Papa, I'm not a baby."

"Yes, you are." Jack swooped her up. He ran with her out into knee-deep water. When he put her down he kicked water at her. Sophia giggled, splashing him right back.

Amin and Miguel waded out to join the fun.

Jack saw a school of silver herring swim toward them in the crystal clear water. "Sophia, don't let the little fishies eat you."

Sophia looked down. They raced by her legs like speeding bullets grazing her skin with their scaly bodies. She looked more surprised than afraid.

Jack watched the synchronized shoal disappear behind a patch reef. He looked further out. Asha and Maria were standing in waist-high water.

Amin walked up to Jack. "Let's go over to the women."

Miguel hoisted Sophia up onto his shoulders. He waded out with Amin and Jack.

"It is best to shuffle your feet in the sand."

"Why's that?" Jack asked Amin.

"So you do not step on them."

"Step on what?"

"You will see."

Maria cried out.

Saucer-like creatures were circling Asha. She stood motionless with her hand extended under the water, holding a sardine. A stingray hovered over her hand for a moment then swam off having eaten the offering.

Jack counted twenty of them. The sea animals undulated gracefully through the water in wave-like motions, some flapping their wing-like fins like birds in flight.

A stingray rested on Asha's outstretched arms. She looked like an animal trainer performing in an aquatic amusement park.

"Aren't they venomous?" Miguel asked Amin.

"They are tame if not threatened. That is why you must slide your feet on the sandy bottom. If you step on one hiding in the sand it will sting you."

The stingrays glided through the water, propelling themselves with their pectoral fins, the claspers and pelvic fins controlling their short tails; each spine equipped with a venomous stinger barb.

Amin looked at Jack. "My wife thinks she is a mermaid."

"I can see that. Think she'd mind if I had a go?"

"She would be delighted."

Jack waded over to Asha, making sure to drag his feet through the sand.

"Ah, Jack. Would you like to feed my friends?"

"Show me what to do."

Asha handed Jack a sardine. "Hold it up by the tail."

A four-foot wide stingray went straight for Jack's hand as soon as he put it under the water. He felt a tug on the sardine as the stingray grabbed it in its mouth. The batoid swam off, joining the circling procession for another turn at a treat.

Jack and Asha took turns feeding the fish. Soon the plastic bag was empty. Asha tucked it in the waistband of her swimsuit.

The fever of stingrays lingered for a few minutes then went off in search of food in deeper waters.

***

The airport shuttle bus was waiting for them when they got back to the house. They threw on some clothes. Jack and Miguel carried out the already packed bags, stowing them in the back of the bus. They took a moment to say goodbye to Amin and Asha, everyone hugging before climbing into the shuttle.

"So where will you be going from here?" Amin asked Jack.

"Madagascar."

25

VOROMPATRA

Jack and Miguel didn't know what was worse, hiking through the sweltering jungles of Indonesia or scrambling in the Madagascan underbrush. Every time they thought they were on a path, scraggily branches would block their way forcing them to use their machetes to carve a trail.

Jack's arm was growing tired from swinging the heavy blade. "I wonder why Nora didn't provide us with a guide?" He took off his baseball cap to wipe his forehead with his arm.

"Probably felt we would do just as well with a GPS tracker." Miguel looked down at the colored screen on his handheld device. The satellite readings had been accurate under the open sky but spotty traveling under the thick canopy.

Jack saw a conspiracy of ring-tailed lemurs observing him and Miguel from the overhead branches with mild interest like bored spectators watching a passing parade. A green gecko racing headfirst down the side of a tree paused suddenly to watch them slicing their way through the jungle. Everywhere Jack turned there was some type of creature monitoring their every move. Even the bothersome gnats got in on the act.

"What do you say we take a little break?" Jack cleaved his machete into the trunk of tree for safekeeping.

"Fine by me." Miguel sat on a log to consult his GPS tracker.

Jack plopped down beside his friend. "So you think this thing really exists or is she sending us on a wild goose chase?"

"If she is, we're after one hell'uva big goose. The vorompatra is supposed to be twice the size of an ostrich. Nora says it could weigh up to a thousand pounds. Probably why it's called the Elephant Bird. Be happy she only wants an egg."

"Which makes us a couple of egg-stealing weasels." Jack stood deciding to shove on. He pulled his machete out of the tree.

"We get lucky this could be a big payday for us and our website."

They continued through the thickets. The going got a little easier as the vegetation began to thin out. Soon they reached an open area overgrown with high grass.

Something cracked under Jack's boot. He lifted his foot. He bent down and picked up a piece of eggshell the size of a cracked dinner plate.

Miguel glanced down at the remnants. "Hopefully there's more where that came from."

They began searching through the grass.

Jack was the first to find an intact egg. He picked it up to show Miguel. It was bigger than a football. "Thing's heavy. Must weigh fifteen, twenty pounds."

"That's one big omelet." Miguel opened the rucksack slung over his shoulder.

Jack was about to put the egg in when he heard something big stampeding through the grass. He looked behind him. Nora hadn't been kidding. The bird was enormous; at least twelve feet tall. It was covered with coarse, gray feathers, resembling an ostrich but with a fuller body and no wings. The powerful red legs were thick as flagpoles with three-toed feet.

The vorompatra inflated its long neck, bellowing an *awking* sound meant to scare them off as it charged through the grass.

Jack tucked the egg under his arm. He dashed back into the brush.

The giant bird sprinted after Jack, its stride surpassing his with remarkable speed.

Running parallel to his friend, Miguel yelled out, "Throw it to me."

Jack glanced over his shoulder. The bird was almost upon him. He did a lateral pass to Miguel.

Miguel curled his arms for a *soft* catch, almost stumbling so as not to drop the fragile egg.

The vorompatra veered after Miguel.

They found themselves back in the thickets, rushing through dense briars. Sharp thorns tore at their faces and arms, ripping their clothes. Jack lashed out with his machete, blazing a path. He glanced over at Miguel. His friend was on his hands and knees crawling through a small opening, rolling the egg on the ground in front of him.

The massive ratite crashed into the impenetrable barrier. It squawked with alarm when large thorns jabbed into its chest and tore at its legs. The more it struggled to get at Miguel, the more it found itself ensnared by the merciless thicket. Finally, the bird gave up, backing out of the entanglement. Its heavy feet stomped back toward the grassland.

Jack chopped his way through the overgrowth until he came out into a small patch where Miguel was waiting, sitting on the ground with the egg. Like Jack, his face and arms were scratched up and bleeding.

"You look like hell."

"At least we got the egg." Miguel reached down to pat the egg.

The egg was gone.

"What the hell? Where'd it go?"

Jack heard something moving behind a tree. He rushed over, spotting what looked like a reddish-brown short-furred cougar with an elongated body like a mongoose. The fossa was six-foot long from its nose to the tip of its tail, weighing at least fifty pounds. It used its front paws to roll the egg along on the ground like a soccer player.

Jack and Miguel raced after the egg-stealer.

The chase didn't last long.

The egg got away from the fossa and went tumbling down an incline. The white spheroid rolled over the edge of a drop-off, disappearing into a ravine choked with overgrown prickly-thorn spinose plants.

The fossa scampered up into a tree.

Jack stared down at the impassable foliage below. "No way am I going down there." He glanced over at the razor-thin slashes on Miguel's face and arms. He looked like a victim of the Chinese slow torture, *lingchi*, known as the death by a thousand cuts.

"Guess Nora's going to have to find something else on the menu for us to find."

26

MYSTERY WOMAN

Jack stepped out of the shower and toweled off. He studied his abrasions in the mirror over the bathroom sink. He didn't look as horrifying as when they had returned to the waterfront hotel. Most of the cuts had been superficial, and once thoroughly rinsed, were nothing but trifle scratches. He applied antiseptic ointment to prevent infections. One cut on his forehead above his right eye required a butterfly bandage.

His clothes were stacked neatly on the toilet seat cover. He pulled on his briefs, and stepped into his jeans. He put on a long-sleeved cotton shirt to cover his lacerated arms. He stepped out of the bathroom and sat down on a chair by the window overlooking the parking lot and the large harbor of moored fishing boats and cargo ships.

Miguel sat at a small table with his laptop. He had already cleaned up; his damp raven black hair combed straight back dripping on the back of his collar. He looked up from the computer screen. "The Wi-Fi here is for the shits. I can't get on the Internet."

"You can try her later. Let's go get something to eat." Jack slipped on his socks.

"Sounds good." Miguel closed up his laptop. He got up from the table, taking his computer.

"You're bringing that along?" Jack finished lacing up his boots and stood.

"I'm not leaving it here."

They locked the room and took the stairs, as the elevator was out of order. If Jack were to evaluate the hotel, he would probably give it a two-star rating. The inside of the building needed repainting and a good cleaning. Every time Jack saw a room service tray outside a hotel door to be picked up, he'd spot cockroaches feeding on bits of food left on the plates. Miguel joked their piss-poor accommodations was a reflection of their inability to meet Nora's quota.

Jack hoped their next assignment—if there was another assignment—was realistically attainable.

Leaving the hotel, they headed over to the boardwalk stretching along the marina with cannery warehouses, tackle shops, seafood restaurants, and waterfront bars. Each time Jack stopped to review a menu posted outside a restaurant, Miguel would shake his head and pull him away.

Finally, Miguel pointed to a sign—*Free Wi-Fi*—posted on the front of a door leading into a bar.

Jack looked up at the neon sign over the door. "Dead Man's Tavern. Somehow that doesn't sound too inviting."

"Come on. I'm sure they have food." Miguel opened the door and stepped inside.

Jack had been in his share of seedy bars, this one being no exception; the gloomy room, the fishy air reeking of stale beer and sweat from bodies toiling the docks. Ship helm wheels along with old nautical gauges and mooring ropes hung on the walls. The bar counter extended down one side of the room, a scuffed picture of a half-naked woman wrapped in a flag painted on the front. Shelves of alcohol bottles lined the back wall glinting under the sparse ceiling lights. A bartender with a long braided beard and a tattoo sleeve on his right arm was filling a beer glass from the tap.

Four men sat at the bar on wooden stools. Their backs were turned, hunched over the bar top. From their clothes they looked like fishermen or maritime sailors.

Six round tables with wooden armrest chairs took up most of the floor.

A woman was sitting at a table in the shadows at the back of the room.

Miguel handed the laptop to Jack. "Go grab us a table."

Besides the bartender, the four at the bar, and the woman, Jack saw no other patrons in the place. "See if they have fish and chips."

"You'll be lucky to get peanuts and pretzels."

Jack sauntered to the rear of the bar. He could feel the soles of his boots sticking to the floor. He didn't want to seem presumptuous by walking up to the woman so he sat at the table next to hers. He put the laptop on the table.

She gave him a sideways glance and stared back down at her drink.

"So what's that you're drinking?"

The woman looked at Jack and scoffed, "What happened to you?"

"What?" He saw her eyes roving his face. "Bad razor."

"Didn't know you guys shaved your foreheads."

"I got a little carried away."

Miguel came up to the table, carrying two glass steins by the handles and a pitcher of beer. He sat down across from Jack. "They don't have a kitchen."

"Not even peanuts?"

Miguel shook his head and began filling the steins.

"Don't tell me you two share the same razor."

Jack turned to the woman. "No, it's more like an occupational hazard."

"Vanilla rum."

"I'm sorry, what?"

"You asked me what I was drinking. Vanilla rum."

"Can I buy you another?"

"I'd be disappointed if you didn't."

Miguel looked at Jack. He gave his friend a sly grin. "You certainly don't want to get a reputation for disappointing women."

"Oh, you mean like Nora?"

"You entertain the lady. I'll go get her drink." Miguel took a swallow of his beer. He got up and went back to the bar.

"So what's this hazardous occupation of yours?" The woman slid her chair closer to Jack's table.

Jack didn't answer right away.

"I doubt you're a lion tamer."

"You would be right."

"I can't imagine you being a cat fancier."

"I'm more a dog person."

Miguel came back with the woman's drink. He smiled, placing the glass in front of her. He sat down with Jack.

"Thank you." The woman took a sip of the rum.

Jack looked over at Miguel. "She wants to know what we do for a living."

"Tell her."

"Seriously?"

"Why not?"

Jack smiled at the woman. "Well, if you must know, we're cryptid hunters."

"You're what?" The woman burst into laughter nearly knocking over her glass.

"No, we are." Jack didn't know if he should be offended but then he, too, started laughing.

"So what, you guys go traipsing through the woods looking for Bigfoot?"

"Well, we haven't quite done that yet."

Miguel opened his laptop. "Here, I'll show you our blog page. The bartender gave me the Wi-Fi password."

The woman picked up her drink. She moved from her table to sit next to Miguel so she could see the computer screen.

Jack scooted his chair next to the woman. His heart began to race as he looked at her beautiful face in the glow of the screen. Green eyes, freckles across the bridge of her nose and cheeks, auburn hair tucked in a tightly weaved ponytail. She seemed genuinely interested in watching Miguel flick from one website to another. Jack saw her expression change when Miguel opened an email from Nora and the Wilde Enterprises logo popped up. She leaned back in her chair.

"Oh, boy. Nora just beeped us on ChatLine." Miguel turned the computer slightly so Jack could see the screen.

Professor Howard appeared on the monitor. She seemed excited. "Thank God I was able to get hold of you. I need you to stop what you're doing as I have a new assignment for you."

Jack saw the relieved look on Miguel's face.

"You will be going to an uncharted island."

"Where?" Jack asked.

Nora read the coordinates from a printout on her desk. Miguel jotted the information down on a notepad.

"What's so special about this island?"

"Watch." A small image popped up of a barren volcanic island surrounded by ocean in the lower right-hand corner of the screen. They watched for two minutes as the bleak brown landmass gradually changed in color to various shades of green.

"How long did that take? Five-ten years?"

"No, Jack. It's not Timelapse Satellite Imagery. That was real time. This was recorded a few weeks ago."

"But that's impossible."

"I believe it's a cryptid event like nothing we have ever seen before."

Jack saw a speck next to the island. "What's that off the shore?"

"A shipwreck."

That piqued the woman's interest. She leaned forward to get a peek at the screen.

"Who's that woman with you?" Nora asked.

The woman sat back in her chair. She looked at Jack, shaking her head.

"Our waitress." Jack playacted and looked over his shoulder. "It's okay. She left."

"So when do we leave?" Miguel asked.

"Tonight. There's a small freight ship at Pier 5: the Dark Horizon. Good luck to you both and keep me posted." Nora's image faded.

"Of course we're leaving tonight," Miguel said in a weary tone.

Jack glanced over at the bar. A sinister-looking man looked in his direction and slid off his stool. A long, white scar extended from his forehead intersecting the patch covering his right eye all the way down his face to his chin like a blade had savagely cleaved him. He started walking towards their table. Jack noticed a circular tattoo on his upper arm that looked like a Mayan medallion with a skull face in the center. He also saw a thin-bladed knife glinting in the man's hand. "Miguel, we got trouble."

The woman saw the man approaching. She stood, kicking back her chair. "Tarik, no!"

"You know this guy?" Jack asked.

Miguel closed up his laptop. "He better not be after my computer."

Jack watched the woman go up to Tarik. He could hear her whispering but couldn't make out what she was saying. Tarik didn't seem too interested in what she had to say and tried to brush past her. She put her hand on his chest, stopping him. She said something in a sterner voice. Whatever it was, it was enough to convince him to back off.

The woman turned to Jack and Miguel. "Thanks for the drink boys."

Jack and Miguel watched as they left the bar.

"What was that? A jealous boyfriend?" Miguel was still staring at the door.

"That guy wasn't her boyfriend."

"So you think it was a con? She sets us up and this jerk hits us when we leave?"

"We better hang tight for a bit."

"I've no problem with that." Miguel grabbed the pitcher and filled their glasses.

27

STOWAWAYS

Laney Moss entered the pirates' den, which was a vacated warehouse on an abandoned pier a short distance from the main harbor. The ancient wood structure was decayed and falling apart with rotted holes in the roof. Waves lapped the pilings rhythmically below the deck boards. Seagulls fluttered in, roosting on the guano-stained rafters.

Twenty or so men sat at tables or together on the floor, cleaning their handguns and semi-automatic rifles in preparation for the next raid. Two grenade launchers were in a crate by the wall along with scores of metal ammo boxes.

Tarik Obob walked in after Laney. He hadn't spoken to her since she had foiled his attempt to rob the two men at the bar. If it had been any other woman, he would have enjoyed beating her to a bloody pulp. But then if he did, he would have sealed his fate, negating a hand or spending the rest of eternity feeding the fish, chained to a piling at the bottom of the bay.

Laney was the property of Butros Jabeen.

Butros sat in a throne-style chair. Behind him was a large window with a crossword puzzle design of smudged and translucent panes allowing a partial view of the setting sun beyond the seaboard. As soon as Butros saw Laney he bellowed, "Ah, my little castaway has returned."

Laney occupied the chair next to the corsair leader.

Butros plucked at his black beard as he often did whenever he was ruminating about strategies for a new incursion. He smiled fondly at Laney, displaying his nicotine-stained horse teeth. He was wearing a Sherpa jacket and a woolen cap.

A two-way radio rested on the armrest of his chair.

On his lap, a Colt .45 semi-automatic pistol with gold inlays on the barrel and handgrip.

Laney watched Tarik approach.

Butros looked up at his second-in-command. "Tarik. You have nothing for me?"

"She stopped me."

Butros turned to Laney. His face was impossible to read.

"He's right. I did," Laney beamed.

"She was with two men," Tarik said. "I think she was conspiring with them."

Butros' right hand rested on the handgrip of his gun. "Most unfortunate."

"No, quite the opposite. Those men Tarik saw me with were treasure hunters."

"Treasure hunters," Butros said dubiously.

"They showed me an island on their computer where there is a shipwreck full of gold bullions."

Butros gazed at Tarik. "Is that so?"

"They were looking at something—"

Laney cut him off. "They are leaving tonight. We could sneak aboard. Take over their ship once we're there."

"She's lying."

"Am I?" Laney smiled at Butros. "I assure you. You will be *very* rich."

"And where is this?"

"Pier 5. The Dark Horizon."

"Tarik, alert the men."

Tarik glared at Laney with his one eye then stormed off.

"Butros, you must promise me one thing," Laney said.

"And what is that, my little castaway?"

"You won't kill anyone."

"Sorry, that I cannot promise."

***

The pirates crept along the dock, keeping to the shadows. They hid behind pallets stacked with cargo. Tarik peered over the lid of a crate. He had a rope coiled over his shoulder with a grappling hook on the end. He watched the seaman patrolling above him, making his rounds on the ship. He waited until the sailor headed back toward the stern.

Tarik ran over to the mooring cleat by the bow of the Dark Horizon. He ducked under the mooring line stretching up to the ship. He grabbed hold of the rope, pulling himself up hand over hand, feet draped over the line. He made his way to the main deck of the ship. He hung the grappling hook on the metal side and threw down the rope.

Two marauders ran toward the ship, scurrying up the ropes. Another pair followed. Then more invaded the ship.

Tarik opened a deck hatch leading down to the forward cargo area. The men snuck down carrying a cache of weapons and small sacks of provisions.

Butros and Laney were last to come on board. Butros detached the grappling hook, letting it splash down into the water. They shimmied down the ladder into the dark hold of the ship.

Tarik stood on the top rungs and sealed the hatch.

28

COMMANDEERED

Jack was bored out of his skull. They'd been out to sea for five days and still no sign of the mysterious island. He was beginning to wonder if it really existed. Standing midsection on the portside, he gazed through the binoculars at the flat water. Instead of focusing on the horizon directly, he scanned just above the horizontal plane, as it was a better way to spot an object on the thin line between the blues of the sky and ocean.

He turned when he heard footsteps approaching.

Miguel leaned over the side to watch the white water skirting past the side of the steel hull. "I talked to the captain."

"Yeah, what did he say?"

"By his calculations we should be sighting the island soon."

"Any more updates from Nora?" Jack raised his binoculars to take another look around.

"I haven't been able to reach her today. There's no satellite signal."

"Maybe the captain will have better luck."

"He says they haven't been able to reach anyone on the ship's radio."

Jack lowered his binoculars and looked at Miguel. "So where are we, the Bermuda Triangle?"

"Well, I don't think we're anywhere near there. It could be anything." Miguel looked up at the flotilla of battleship-gray clouds moving in their direction. "Could be those clouds causing the interference."

"Or we're entering dark waters."

"What are you gibbering about? Can I see those?"

Jack removed the lanyard around his neck and handed Miguel the binoculars.

"You know, like the Sargasso Sea."

Miguel held the binoculars up to his eyes. “If my memory serves me isn’t that where they found ships adrift with their crews missing?”

“That’s right.”

“And weren’t they supposed to have been eaten by some carnivorous seaweed?”

“Right again.”

Miguel handed the binoculars back to Jack. “Do you see any seaweed?”

Jack looked over the side and saw nothing but blue ocean.

“I don’t think we have anything to worry about.”

A man yelled further up near the bow, followed by a gunshot.

Jack looked at Miguel. “You were saying?”

They heard more gunfire.

“What do you think, a mutiny?”

“Whatever it is, I don’t think we want to get caught in the middle. Not without our guns.” Jack and Miguel ran for the nearest access hatch and slipped inside. They ran down the passage, sliding down the ladder railing to the level below. Jack flung his cabin door open and went in while Miguel entered his stateroom.

They stepped back into the passageway. Jack strapped on his gun belt. He checked the open cylinder on his Colt .44 Magnum revolver and snapped it shut. Miguel slung on his shoulder rig. He pulled back the slide on his .357 Desert Eagle semi-automatic pistol, inserting a round into the chamber.

“Where’s your laptop?”

“Hidden where no one will find it,” Miguel said.

“Let’s go see what this is all about.”

They had just reached the base of the ladder steps when a crewmember suddenly appeared on the landing above. He saw Jack and Miguel and yelled, “They’re attacking the ship.”

“Who is?” Jack yelled up.

A man came up behind the sailor. He reached around the front of the frightened mariner and slit his throat with one clean sweep. Blood spurted out the thin gash, splattering the bulkhead and splashing down on the steps.

The knife-wielding killer pushed the bleeding man down the metal stairwell.

Miguel stepped to the side so as not to be bowled over by the tumbling body. He fired two quick rounds at the murderer.

The man above dropped on the deck.

Jack and Miguel charged up the steps.

They stood over the dead man, staring at his face.

"I don't remember this guy when the captain took us around and introduced us to his crew," Miguel said.

"Me neither." Jack saw a Mayan medallion with a skull face in the center on the man's arm. "I saw the same tattoo on that guy in the bar."

They heard men yelling and screaming outside.

"What the hell's going on out there?"

"My guess, we're being attacked by pirates." Jack crept over to the hatch leading outside. As soon as he stepped out on the deck, a man came running at him. He was screaming, holding a bloody stump where his hand used to be. He was so hysterical he kept running after he passed Jack and Miguel.

Another man came racing down the deck, holding a blood-dripping machete above his head.

Jack shot him three times.

The pirate stumbled, dropping the machete. He slammed into the railing, his momentum catapulting him over the side.

Jack and Miguel ran forward. The main deck near the bow was swarming with pirates. More were climbing out of a cargo bay hatch like sewer rats. Some of the ship's crew, including the ship's captain, were on their knees with their hands behind their heads. Jack counted three dead, their dismembered bodies lying in large pools of blood.

The barbarians laughed as if the atrocity of brutally hacking up another human being meant nothing to them.

Jack saw a heathen climbing a ladder to a lookout post near the top of a mast.

A dozen men pointed their automatic rifles at Jack and Miguel.

"What now?" Miguel asked Jack.

"Maybe we can reason with them."

"I don't think that's going to work. Look what they're doing to the crew."

Jack saw the man with the eye patch. "Ah, shit. That's the guy from the bar. What did she call him?"

"Tarik."

The men stood in firing squad formation waiting on Tarik's command.

A burly man with a black beard exited the cargo hatch. He stood over the opening and extended his hand. He assisted a slender figure onto the deck.

"I don't believe it," Jack said. "It's the woman from the bar."

As soon as she saw Jack and Miguel she immediately said to the man beside her, "Butros, those are the men."

"If you want to live, I suggest you drop your guns." Butros lit a cheroot and blew out a steady stream of smoke. "The choice is entirely up to you."

"Maybe we can talk our way out of this." Jack lowered his gun. He bent down and laid his revolver on the deck. Miguel did the same.

A pirate confiscated their weapons.

"So, I gather you are the treasure hunters?" Butros said.

"What?" Jack looked at Miguel. He could see his friend was also drawing a blank.

The woman stepped forward. "If you show us where the gold is, Butros will spare your lives."

"I'm sorry. Who are you?"

"My name is Laney Moss. Do as they say and no harm will come to you."

"Maybe we had too many beers that night. Can you kindly refresh my memory?"

"The shipwreck on your computer. The one with the treasure."

"Okay," Jack said, still not getting her meaning but eager to stall as long as possible.

Laney came closer until she was standing a foot away from Jack and Miguel. She whispered so the others couldn't hear, "Are you thick? Play along."

Tarik looked at Laney suspiciously then turned to his boss. "Why do we need two when one can lead us to the gold?"

Butros puffed on his cigar, giving his second-in-command a shrug.

Tarik waved two men over. They tied Jack and Miguel's hands behind their backs.

"I'm not liking this," Jack said to Miguel.

"What are they going to do, make us walk the plank?"

Tarik must have overhead Miguel because he said, "There are worse ways to die."

"Please, Butros," Laney pleaded. "Don't let Tarik do this."

"It amuses me. Besides, what else is there to do?"

Jack watched a few pirates hurry away. They came back with planks and crates and built a scaffold next to the ship's railing.

Tarik ordered his men to force three crewmembers with their hands bound behind their backs onto the scaffolding. They stood, heels to the edge of the railing. One step back and it was over the side into the ocean below.

A pirate handed Tarik a long gaff with a six-foot long shaft.

Tarik walked up to the first man. He jabbed the barbed spear into the man's chest, shoving him backwards over the side. The man screamed all the way down before striking the water. The second man begged for his life only to be prodded over the railing. The third man tried to jump off the plank. In his panic, he tripped over his own feet and plummeted down the side of the ship.

Jack and Miguel were hoisted onto the plank.

"Butros, what are you doing?" Laney said to the corsair leader.

"Like Tarik said. We only need one."

"Please, don't—"

"If it will make you feel better, you may choose."

"No, I can't do that."

"You may proceed," Butros told Tarik.

Tarik placed the tip of the gaff against Miguel's chest.

"He has a wife and a daughter," Jack yelled. "Pick me instead."

"Jack, shut up. I got the short straw. It's okay."

"Think of Maria and Sophia."

Butros stepped in front of the scaffold. "It is noble to want to die for one's friend." He turned to Tarik. "Don't you agree?"

Tarik applied more pressure on the gaff, pushing Miguel back so his heels were hanging over the plank.

"No, stop!" Jack screamed. He gazed up and saw the pirate up on the lookout post pointing at something off the forward bow.

"Land Ho!"

PART THREE

THE ISLAND

29

LANDING PARTY

The Dark Horizon anchored a half-mile offshore from the island. Storm winds churned the once-tranquil sea into furrows of white-capped swells. A light rain pelted the pirates as they lowered the two launches into the water. Rope ladders stretched down to the boats for boarding. None of the ship's crew was among the landing party as Butros had ordered them and the captain confined to the bridge under heavy guard.

Tarik was in charge of the first boat with six of his men. Jack and Miguel sat side by side in the middle of the craft, their hands no longer tied. Two pirates watched them intently with their guns. Jack glanced back at the second boat. Eight men accompanied Butros and Laney as they got underway.

Facing forward in the boat, Jack had a view of the island and the shipwreck cast upon the rocks. There were places where the steel hull was exposed under scant patches of overlaying foliage. He didn't see barnacles or moss growing on the metal; just overgrown leafy vines, which might have suggested the wreckage had been there for years instead of only a few weeks.

He heard shorebirds keening above. Leaning back, he gazed up into the overcast sky expecting to see white seagulls soaring overhead. He nudged Miguel to look up. "What do you make of those?"

Miguel stared at the birds. "You got to be kidding me. Flying peacocks?"

"But they're too small. And besides, peacocks don't fly." Jack watched the small flock of colorful birds fly in a circular pattern above their boat. A shorebird split away from the group and swooped down over the boat. A pirate stood, striking the bird with a neck-snapping wallop with the butt of his rifle, killing it. The gull fell into the water.

Jack leaned over the gunwale to get a closer glimpse of the dead bird with its wings spread open, floating on its back in an undulating trough. Like its head and body, the wings were multi-shades of different colors as if an artist stirred together his entire palette and created a universal template for the entire spectrum.

Before the bird sank from view, Jack swore he saw it revive, its feathered body transforming into some type of aquatic kelp-like creature. "Jesus, what the—"

"What's wrong?" Miguel asked.

"I must be seeing things."

"Shut up," growled a pirate. He jiggled the barrel of his gun at Jack and Miguel.

Tarik stood up on the forward thwart. He pointed to a flat boulder jutting out from behind the centerline of the shipwreck's bow. "Bring her around. We will board from there."

The two men rowing propelled the launch one last time, pulling the oars in through the crutches. The man at the tiller cut the rudder hard to the right so the boat wouldn't smack into the rocks.

Tarik looked down at Jack and Miguel. "Now you take us to the gold."

Everyone piled out of the boat except for the tillerman. They clambered over the slippery boulders wet from the ocean spray of the pounding waves—a preamble to the storm to come.

Jack gazed out over the choppy water. Butros' launch was a hundred yards away, riding the rolling surf toward the black sandy beach to wait it out while Tarik and his men searched the wreckage.

Miguel turned and whispered to Jack, "What do we do when they realize there's no gold?"

"We better have something good up our sleeves."

Tarik chose his smallest man to go up first to test the strength of the vines covering the side of the wreckage. The man grabbed a thick vine and began scaling the ivy like a Marine working his way up a rope climb on an obstacle course. Tarik watched the pirate get halfway up then turned to signal another man to follow.

"Aaargh!"

Jack gazed up at the man twenty feet above his head. Green serpents—big around as garden hoses—were wrapping around the man's torso and legs. He struggled to pull back his arm but his wrist was seized, flipping him around onto his back.

"Snakes?" Tarik yelled at Jack and Miguel. "Is this one of your tricks?"

"They're not snakes," Jack said. "Those are strangler vines."

A vine coiled around the man's neck like a hangman's noose. His face turned from beet-red to a dark purple as his windpipe was crushed. The vines cinched tightly around his body holding him against the side of the ship like a crucifixion. More vines crisscrossed his body until he was completely concealed under the leaves.

"What is this place?" Miguel asked Jack.

"Jesus, why the hell would she send us here?"

Tarik glared at Jack and Miguel. "You led us into a trap."

"If it was, we didn't know about it."

"We had no idea," Miguel said, raising his hands in his defense.

The rain came down harder, the heavy pellets ricocheting off the rocks. A leeward wind howled over the turbulent sea sending waves crashing onto the shore. Jack knew it would be impossible to row back to the ship against the strong current. Their only hope of shelter was the island. He looked across the water, spotting the other launch beached on the shore.

There was no sign of Laney, Butros or any of his men.

"Back to the boat," Tarik yelled.

They climbed cautiously down the wet rocks in the buffeting wind.

The man in the launch was using an oar to keep the pitching boat from dashing against the boulders by the raging waves. A huge swell lifted the stern ten feet up, spilling the man over the side. The man came to the surface just as the keel came crashing down on the top of his head.

Two men shimmied down the rocks to grab hold of the boat. A sidelong wave pushed the launch beyond their reach. The dory continued to drift farther away. A powerful comber rolled over the boat, capsizing the vessel.

Jack watched the next set of waves pour over the launch, sinking their one chance of returning to the Dark Horizon.

Tarik cursed their misfortune. He began leading the group over the rocks toward the beach. Two pirates followed right behind, the other two taking up the rear with their guns trained on Jack and Miguel.

With the torrential rain beating down on them and the chilling wind cutting them to the bone, Jack wished they'd had the foresight to bring foul weather gear. It was like standing under a bathroom shower, fully dressed.

Hunched over, they stumbled through the deluge. Once they reached the beach, the rainforest was only a hundred feet away. Jack was amazed how tall the trees had grown in such a short period of time. The canopy sloping up the mountain had to be a hundred feet up from the jungle floor.

Their boots crunched across the pebbly basalt rock.

Jack caught a white, thin flash out of the corner of his eye. At first, he thought it was the wind slanting the rain, but then he saw another similar image a few feet away in the other direction. A pirate walking in front of him saw it as well. He let out a cry of alarm, frightened by the strange sight.

Soon, swift-moving objects were zipping all around them like fluorescent dive-bombers.

"The island is possessed," a pirate yelled.

Tarik pulled his machete from the sheath on his belt. He swung at a passing sliver of light, missing it entirely as it zipped in another direction. "What are these things?"

"My guess," Jack said. "They're air rods."

An air rod landed on a pirate's wrist. He glanced down at the winged centipede; its six-inch long body translucent like a ghost. It raced up his arm onto his shoulder and burrowed into his ear. The man screamed, attracting scores of air rods to light upon him like iron filings drawn to a magnet. The specters slithered up the man's nostrils and into his wailing mouth, scrabbling into every orifice.

"We have to get off this beach." Jack and Miguel ran toward the edge of the jungle. Tarik and the three remaining freebooters dashed after them in the torrential rain.

Jack turned to Miguel. "Those air rods must have scared off Butros and his men."

"Could be these pirates spook easy."

"Something we could use to our advantage."

They darted between the thick fronds into the jungle.

30

PELUDA

As they ran through the dense vegetation, Jack couldn't help noticing the plants and trees were unlike any he had ever seen. Giant twenty-foot tall ferns in the shrub layer stretched up into the palms below the evergreen treetops shrouded in misty clouds. The high canopy served as an umbrella shielding them from the fierce downpour as the rainwater funneled down the leaves and epiphytes sprouting earthward on tree trunks tapering to the forest floor when they should have been narrowing skyward.

Jack spotted creeper plants clinging to tree branches with exposed roots moving about like tiny octopi tentacles snatching windblown food particles out of thin air. He passed humongous flowers with petals three-feet in diameter, ripe with pollen.

"Stop!" Tarik yelled.

Jack and Miguel came to a crashing halt in a small clearing. Tarik and the three men caught up and staggered around them. Standing under the luxuriant foliage, they took a moment to catch their breath having run nearly half a mile inland without stopping. The rain and wind had eased up so it was much quieter—like being in the eye of a hurricane—than when they were on the beach being assaulted by the storm.

Jack looked back in the direction they had come from. It was impossible to tell where they rudely blazed a path. The trampled plants and broken branches had re-established to their original shapes.

At least they had outrun the dreadful air rods.

Everyone turned to a soft fluttering sound coming from one of the enormous flowers. A pirate raised his machete.

"Don't kill it. It's harmless," Jack shouted at the man.

"My God it's huge," Miguel said.

Jack took a couple of steps toward the massive flower. "It's a mega moth." He watched the giant moth unfurl its 18-inch long proboscis down the throat of the plant to gather up nectar. The large insect must have sensed Jack's encroaching presence as it took flight and disappeared into the trees.

A figure pushed aside a huge rattan palm leaf to step into the clearing. It was Butros. He pulled Laney in with him. Seven pirates came in as well.

"Where are your other men?" Butros asked Tarik.

"Three are dead."

"As is one of mine. By those strange creatures on the beach."

"Air rods," Jack said, thinking the corsair might be curious what killed his men and made them run for their lives like frightened rabbits.

Butros nodded like he already knew.

A huge beast the size of a water buffalo charged into the clearing. It looked like a dragon with a slender neck, short reptilian legs, a long tail, and a back carpeted with tightly woven green hairs.

"Kill the monster," Tarik yelled.

The pirates with automatic rifles aimed their weapons.

Jack recognized the creature from their cryptozoology chart.

It was a Peluda.

When threatened, those hairs on its back became deadly projectile stingers like the quills on a porcupine.

"Hit the dirt!" Jack and the others dove onto the ground to the sound of a hundred archers releasing their arrows. The deadly spines ripped through the palms, imbedding into tree trunks. Jack saw a man impaled in the face and chest fall to the ground. He looked like an unfortunate patient from an acupuncture session gone terribly wrong.

Three men fired their machineguns at the creature, riddling its body and head with a steady barrage. The Peluda bellowed with pain before slamming onto the wet earth.

Everyone got up.

Butros and Tarik looked around at the remaining men still alive. Laney stepped away from Butros to get closer to Jack while Miguel went over to examine the slain cryptid.

Jack noticed the dead man on the ground was wearing his gun belt. He walked over and knelt beside the body. He began to unbuckle the belt strap.

"What are you doing?" Tarik growled.

"Getting my gun."

Tarik removed the pistol from his waistband. "You do and you die."

Jack looked at Butros. "If you haven't noticed your men are dropping like flies. You're going to need all the guns you can get if you want to get out of here alive."

"And why should I trust you?"

"Because Miguel and I are your only chance of surviving this place. I don't know what Laney told you but we're not treasure hunters. We're crytpid hunters."

Butros stared at Laney. "You lied to me."

"Not exactly," Laney said. "A rare animal could bring a fortune."

"So you have seen these monsters before?" Butros asked Jack, motioning to the dead creature.

"To be honest, this is our first Peluda. But we're familar with other species."

Miguel waved his arm. "Jack, come here. You have to see this."

Jack stood, not bothering with the gun belt on the dead body. He walked over and stood next to his friend. "What the hell?"

The others milled around the bizarre beast.

"Oh my God," Laney gasped.

The Peluda's body was deflating like a balloon animal with a fast leak. As the neck and legs flattened, thousands of threadlike filaments emerged from the scaly skin to root into the soil. Gradually, the cellular structure of the animal became twining wisps of vegetation. In less than a minute's time, the massive creature was transformed into a large clump of ferns clustered with liverworts.

"I do believe we have just witnessed the Cycle of Life," Jack said.

31

NANDI BEARS

After some haggling, Jack finally convinced Butros to give him and Miguel back their weapons. The pirate with Miguel's Desert Eagle was reluctant to surrender the handgun but was more afraid of what Butros might do to him if he chose to disobey his boss. Jack was grateful there was no argument from the man that wore his gun.

As no one had a compass and it was impossible to get a reading on the position of the sun blocked by the canopy of trees, they found themselves completely lost in the jungle.

"It's an island for God's sake," Miguel said. "Pick a direction. Sooner or later we're going to end up reaching the shore."

"I wish it were that easy." Jack pointed straight ahead at a tunnel in the dense foliage that looked like it had been bored through to forge a trail. No sooner were they a few feet away, the vegetation closed off the path. Another passage opened up inviting them to turn in a different direction.

"This place has us going in circles," Tarik groaned.

Jack had to agree. It was like the island was manipulating their every move; guiding them purposely to a predetermined destination. He saw a break in the trees. The pathway opened up into a small meadow surrounded by marshland. Large shellfish clung to the nearby rocks at the edge of the swamp.

"What are those?" Butros asked.

Jack recalled the cryptozoology chart. "Giant trilobites." The marine arthropods looked like flattened footballs with a series of ridged plates along their backs. Sensing danger, a few skittered into the bog on short jointed legs while others stayed perfectly still to avoid detection though they were out in the open.

"We can use them for food," Tarik instructed the men. The pirates snuck across the short grass. The trilobites must have felt the vibrations of their footsteps because every creature scampered away. The scallywags gave chase even though the trilobites were evasively quicker.

Something swooped down from the trees. Jack ducked thinking it was a bird of prey. When it buzzed over his head he realized it was a giant dragonfly with a five-foot wide wingspan. "Miguel, get a look at that."

"Where are these creatures coming from?"

"I don't know."

"Don't you think it's strange how this island evolved in such a short period of time? What's causing it?"

Laney approached Jack. She made sure Butros and Tarik were preoccupied watching the men chase after the creatures. "I know. It's why I brought us here."

"Care to explain?" Jack asked.

"I believe my husband created all of this."

"Your husband? But how?"

Before Laney could answer, a loud roar interrupted her.

Jack saw the men racing back. Behind them were three beasts that looked like massive hyenas with long front legs and shorter hind legs. They had brown fur over most of their bodies with white on their chests down to their bellies. Their heads were conical-shaped with moose-like ears. "Oh my God. It's a sleuth of Nandi Bears."

The creatures charged after the fleeing men. With a powerful swipe of its front leg, a Nandi Bear cuffed a man with its claws, ripping open the side of his face. As soon as the man fell to the ground, the beast was on top of him. It cracked open the top of the man's skull with its mighty jaws and tore out the brain between its clenched teeth.

Laney stood behind Jack and Miguel as they opened fire on a Nandi Bear running towards them. It took six rounds to bring the creature down.

A man screamed as he was being attacked. He rolled on the ground to escape the cryptid, crawling away on his hands and knees. A fierce chomp severed his head from his shoulders. Automatic gunfire took down the beast. The lone Nandi Bear turned tail and galloped across the meadow into the far jungle. Butros and Tarik went over to make sure the two animals were dead, shooting each one in the head.

Jack glanced over at Laney. "So, are you saying your husband is on this island?"

"Yes."

"Where?"

"Everywhere."

32

DEATH FLOWER

As nightfall approached, Butros told his men to set up camp. Jack, Miguel, and Laney went around collecting anything that might fuel a campfire. They had trouble finding combustible material at first, as everything was either too wet or too green to burn. Eventually they gathered up enough kindling to start a small fire.

The pirates discovered a grove of bamboo nearby. They set to work and came back with armloads of chopped stalks. Soon everyone was sitting around two raging campfires.

Butros, Tarik, and some of the pirates grouped around one campfire, while Jack, Miguel, Laney and a couple of Butros' men warmed themselves by the other fire. The two pirates on the other side of the flames were playing a variation of mumblety-peg with pocketknives. Instead of seeing how close they could come without striking their toes, they were flipping their blades at leaves arranged on the dirt like a game board. They didn't look in Jack's direction, as they were too busy with their game.

"So what did you mean when you said your husband is everywhere?" Jack asked Laney.

"I meant he could be anywhere."

Miguel threw a bamboo stalk into the fire causing the flames to spike with a loud crackling noise. "Can he get us off this island?"

"I doubt it. He's as stranded as we are. I am thirsty."

"Come on, I'll fix you right up." Jack and Laney stood. Jack grabbed a machete lying next to a small pile of bamboo stalks. They walked over to a cluster of long-stemmed vines hanging from a tree. Jack held a liana with one hand and whacked off the end with the machete.

Laney got underneath and let the captured rainwater flow into her mouth. "Hmm, that's good."

Jack pulled the vine toward him. He stood like a kid drinking out of the garden hose. He heard three pirates returning from a hunt. They had managed to find a variety of creatures to cook over the fire, none of which looked especially appetizing.

"Oh my God, we're going to eat that?" Laney groaned.

One man was dragging a giant six-foot long skink along the ground by its right front leg. The tail was missing on the black salamander. Jack figured the man must have tried to grab it by the tail and the appendage broke off; a defense mechanism that might have enabled the reptile to escape if it hadn't been caught.

A pirate carried an enormous snail the size of a basketball. The third man had pieces of what looked like parts of a large insect but it was impossible to tell what it was, only that it looked revolting.

An hour later everyone was through eating. The picked bones of the skink were thrown into the campfires.

Jack tossed his leaf he had used as a plate into the flames. "You know, I was never much for escargot but I have to say that wasn't bad."

"You'll eat anything if you're hungry enough," Miguel said.

Laney made a face. She tossed her untouched piece of snail into the fire. "I think I'm going to hold out for something a little tastier."

"Did you try the salamander?"

"Lizard, yuk."

"Try it. I have a little left over."

Laney looked at the morsel being offered by Jack.

"Is it gamy?"

"Not at all. Sort of tastes like chicken."

"Hell, to you Jack, everything tastes like chicken," Miguel quipped.

Laney took a nibble. "You're right. It does taste like chicken." She gobbled it down.

Tarik walked over. "Three men will guard the camp while we sleep."

"Miguel and I will take turns," Jack told him.

"Butros wants the woman with him."

"Tell Butros she would prefer to stay with us."

Tarik stared at Jack. It was obvious he wasn't going to budge, not until Laney accompanied him.

"It's all right, Jack. Butros doesn't know the meaning of the word *compromise*." Laney got up and walked away with Tarik.

"You could have put up more of a fight," Miguel said.

"Better not to push our luck. We better get some shut eye before our watch comes up." Jack and Miguel lay down by the fire to keep warm. The two pirates sharing their campfire were through playing their game and had retired. One man was using the large petals of a huge flower like a sleeping bag.

Jack closed his eyes and drifted off.

Sometime in the night, a man shouted waking everyone up.

Jack and Miguel sprang to their feet.

It was the man sharing their campfire making all the noise. He was pointing to the man wrapped in the giant flower petals. He was shouting for the sleeping man to wake up but he couldn't respond, as he was already dead, shriveled up like an Egyptian mummy.

Jack could hear slurping along with the sound of liquid flowing down a tube. "I don't believe it. That damn plant's liquefying his body with enzymes and absorbing him."

Tarik marched over with a burning torch. He threw it onto the withered corpse creating a raging funeral pyre. An agonizing wail screeched from the rising blaze.

"My God, that came from the plant," Miguel said.

"Since when do plants scream?"

"They do here."

33

DEVIL TREE

Jack woke up to slivers of blue in the mist-shrouded treetops meaning the storm had finally passed. He could hear Butros and Tarik in a harsh debate. Butros turned away from Tarik and began barking orders to the remaining pirates.

When Jack sat up, he saw Miguel and Laney standing next to the campfire, now a ring of gray ash. "What's all the hollering?"

"Butros is so desperate to get off this island, he's promised the man that leads us back to the beach second-in-command," Miguel said.

"I take it Tarik wasn't too pleased."

"He threatened to kill any man that tried."

"Looks like we might have a bit of a rebellion brewing," Laney grinned.

"You know, the only way we're going to leave this island is on that launch."

"Think it survived the storm?"

"We better hope so." Jack stood and stretched his arms over his head.

"So what side of the island do you think we landed?" Laney asked.

"Well, we were heading due east when the island was spotted. That would mean the launch is on the westerly side."

Miguel looked up at the sunlight filtering down through the fog. "Which means that way is east. So we need to go in the opposite direction."

Jack waved for Tarik to come over.

The man was clearly still angry from talking with Butros. The scar down his flushed face was a shade paler than the rest of his skin.

"We're pretty sure the boat is that way," Jack said, pointing at the jungle in the general direction he believed was west.

"Is this another one of your tricks?" Tarik rested his hand on the grip of his pistol tucked in his waistband.

"Hey, we want to get off the island just as much as you do. I swear, no tricks." Jack saw Butros standing off by a tree, speaking to the larger of the pirates, possibly his favored choice for a new right-hand adjutant.

Tarik watched Butros conspiring with the other man.

"Looks like Butros already has your replacement."

"Shut up or I'll cut out your tongue!"

"Maybe it's time we formed an alliance, what do you say?" Miguel said to Tarik.

Tarik looked at Laney. "It's time for Butros to go."

"No skin off my nose." Laney smiled at the one-eyed pirate.

"Let's tell Butros and get moving." Jack walked over and spoke briefly with Butros, convincing him that he and Miguel knew the proper way back to the beach.

Miguel gazed up into the trees to get a bearing on the sun. Once he was certain, he signaled for everyone to follow him into the jungle.

None of the terrain seemed familiar as they forged through the undergrowth labyrinth. It was like the rainforest had reconstituted itself into a different landscape just to confuse them.

After half an hour of trudging through the seemingly impenetrable foliage, the sweaty and tired group caught a break when Miguel cut down a large palm leaf in his path and stepped into a garden setting of tall tubular plants and a mammoth ominous-looking tree.

Jack spotted succulent fruit hanging on the lower branches that looked like giant raspberries the size of a man's shoe. Each orb of sweet fruit was framed with a hypha, a filamentous fungus.

"Watch out," Miguel yelled, pulling Laney down with him.

Something buzzed over Jack's head. He turned and saw a dobsonfly land on the lip of a pitcher plant. The three-foot long insect had large transparent wings and slightly curved mandibles resembling ice tongs. The bug ventured too far over the rim and slipped into the pitfall trap. A large leaf on the side of the plant came down over the entrance, sealing the insect inside.

Looking around, Jack saw vibrant red plants that looked like huge butterflies with spikes along the ridges of their wings; a mutant strain of Venus flytrap. He whiffed a musty smell. He looked down and saw yellow butterworts with baited insects caught in their sticky leaves.

"This is really creepy," Laney said. "Let's get out of here."

"Not until my men gather fruit." Butros signaled for his men to climb the tree.

Jack turned to Butros. "That might not be a good idea. You better call them back."

"Be quiet. Or I'll—"

"Yeah, I know. You'll cut out my tongue."

Miguel looked at Jack. "I've seen pictures of this tree on Nora's website. That's a devil tree."

Butros looked at Jack and Miguel and started to belly laugh. "A devil..." He couldn't stop howling.

Jack saw a man balanced on a bough, about to reach through the center of a hypha to grab the large berry on the other side. "No, don't put your—"

The fungus cinched around the man's arm causing him to yelp with pain. He screamed louder as the hypha tightened even more, cutting through the flesh down to the bone. The man's arm dropped off and fell to the ground. He passed out, landing next to his severed arm. Roots sprouted out of the ground soaking up the pooling blood.

Another man up in the tree saw what happened and tried to climb down. As soon as he grabbed a branch the gnarled wood forced him against the trunk. More branches seized the man like giant skeletal fingers.

"Oh my God," Laney said stepping away from the malevolent tree.

Jack saw a section of the trunk split open into a gaping maw. "Oh you got to be kidding me." The branches shoved the man inside the tree. The man's bones snapped, as he was crammed into the hollow. The bark closed over the hole. Jack could hear the muffled screams of the man trapped inside. He turned to Miguel standing a couple of feet away. He'd never seen his friend so terrified. Someone was missing. "Where's Laney?"

Miguel glanced around. "She was standing right here."

Jack saw a six-foot tall pitcher plant closing its leaves. "Oh my God!" He grabbed a machete from a pirate staring up at the devil tree. The man didn't even react he was so frightened. Jack ran up to the carnivorous plant and began hacking at the thick, fibrous leaves tough as cow leather.

Miguel joined him with his own machete. The two kept swinging their blades, chopping away the leaves sealing the top. Once the opening was big enough, Jack peeked down the throat of the plant.

"Do you see her?" Miguel asked.

"No, she's gone. But I see light."

"Light from where?"

"There's an underground tunnel."

34

REUNITED

Laney didn't know if she was awake or dreaming. She was floating down a passageway aglow with luminous lichen. It was like staring up at a mystical tapestry under a blue light, the phosphorous greens and blues bright as chemiluminescent glow sticks.

She closed her eyes trying to remember what happened. She'd been watching the man consumed by the tree—*certainly that had been a dream*—when a spore puffball blew into her face from a giant plant. Once she inhaled, she'd found herself drifting into a euphoric state. Looking down, Laney saw she was standing in the center of an enormous flower twelve feet in diameter, its petals spread open upon the ground.

Then the leaves on the corolla rose all around her, capturing her inside as the ground dropped out from under her.

Laney felt her body being lowered onto a soft spongy bed. She opened her eyes. A strange but familiar face gazed down at her. "Hi, Laney."

"Allen?"

"Yes, it's me, in the flesh. Well, maybe not in the flesh. A lot has happened since you last saw me."

Laney didn't comment right away; there was too much to process. Her husband was no longer physically the man she had married. She'd been at his side during the early stages of his transformation but nothing prepared her for what had become of the man she loved.

Allen's form was ethereal, constantly in motion. He was no longer human though the peat moss where his face should be did strike a semblance to that of Allen whenever it morphed, much like an ever-changing Rorschach inkblot image. His shape was covered with glistening green seaweed and dark crusted lichen. He looked like a cross between a primordial creature that had crawled out of the ocean and an aquatic space alien.

Laney was reduced to tears. "Oh, Allen."

"Am I that hideous?"

"No. I just wasn't..." She stopped crying and sucked in a deep breath. She sat up in the bed of strawflowers. She swung her feet onto the ground and stood.

"Sorry. Let me change," Allen said matter of factly like he was simply going off into a bedroom to change his clothes.

Laney watched Allen shapeshift into a somewhat humanistic form.

"Is that better?" he asked.

"Thank you."

"You're welcome. So, what do you think of my island?"

"You did all this?"

"Well, I can't take credit for the rock but I supplied the rest."

"You created all of this in less than one day?"

"Yep. Makes that a new Guinness world record."

Laney heard flapping wings coming down the cavern. She was surprised when a small flamboyant bird landed on Allen's shoulder. "So you have a pet?"

"Well, I guess you can say he's ours really. I call him Star for Starburst the candies." The bird had the same coloring if a confectioner had blended the strawberry, cherry, orange, and lemon taffy together.

"I've never seen a bird like that before."

"I made some slight modifications."

"I'd say those creatures in the jungle are much more than that. Where'd you find them?"

"Caged in the cargo hold. They were normal before I released them."

"What did you do to them?"

"You might say I got a little overzealous."

Laney's clothes clung to her skin from the high humidity inside the cavern. She could hear escaping steam warming and misting the subterranean den like a greenhouse.

Heavy footfalls pounded down the tunneled grotto. Laney saw figures approaching in the luminous passage. It was Jack and Miguel.

"Laney, we thought you were dead." Jack gave her a smile then stopped dead in his tracks when he saw Allen who at the moment was soaking the water vapor from the air and swelling like a giant human-shaped sponge.

"It's okay, don't be alarmed," Laney said.

"Is that..."

"Yes, this is my husband. Allen Moss."

Miguel took a step closer to get a better look at Allen. "How did this happen?"

"It's a long story," Allen replied. "One I'm guessing Laney never told you."

Laney cringed when she heard more footsteps coming. Butros and Tarik strode towards her, followed by the last four pirates.

A pirate leveled the barrel of his assault rifle at Allen. Laney immediately stepped between the gunman and her husband. "Butros, tell him to put down his gun."

Butros was too enthralled by the strange entity standing next to Laney to answer.

"It is the island devil," the pirate said with a voice filled with fear. He sidestepped to get a clear shot.

"Laney, move away before you get hurt." Allen pulled Laney back to push her out of harm's way. Jack grabbed Laney and drew her towards him.

"Tell your man to stand down," Miguel told Butros.

Allen extended his hand in a peaceful gesture.

The pirate pulled the trigger, firing off a short burst into Allen's chest. Some of the bullets exited out his back, pelting the cavern wall.

"I wish you hadn't done that." Allen peeled back a layer of epidermis from his chest revealing a network of chloroplast cells and nutrient transport veins commonplace to a plant. He poked a green finger into his permeable self, plucked out a slug, and flicked it blasely at the pirate.

The cavern rumbled before the metal ball hit the ground.

35

EARTHSHATTERING

Laney clung to Jack as the ground trembled. Sections of rock jarred loose, separating from the cavern walls. A hail of stone fell on a pirate crushing him under a large cloud of billowing dust.

"Not the best place to be in an earthquake," Miguel yelled, covering his head with his hands as chunks of ceiling rained down.

"I'm afraid this is more than a tremor," Allen said. "I think my little island is about to blow." Star squawked, digging its talons into Allen's shoulder.

A fissure opened up fifty feet away on the tunnel floor. Hot, steaming magma bubbled up into a fiery slow-moving lavaflow.

"How do we get out of here?" Jack yelled.

Allen grabbed Laney by the hand. "This way!"

They ran down the stone corridor. Already the temperature was rising, the heat becoming unbearable as the molten ground created a wave of suffocating ash.

Laney was relieved to see sunlight at the end of the tunnel. Racing out the vent hole, she heard a massive explosion like a mega-ton bomb erupting over her head. She could see the highest peak on the island beyond the treetops. A long column of smoke and ash spewed hundreds of feet into the sky. Thousand-degree lava poured out of the volcano in tributary rivers, scorching the highland rainforest. Firestorms swept rapidly down the mountainside.

She glanced over her shoulder. Jack and Miguel were right behind her and Allen. She saw the ground open up. Butros and Tarik jumped over the crevasse. Two pirates made it across. The third pirate attempted the leap but come up short, clawing the edge of the rift for a split second before falling into the chasm.

Every time they came to an impenetrable wall of foliage, the plants and trees would open up a path for Allen. Laney heard what she thought was a jet engine. When she looked up, she saw a volcanic fireball smash into the trees.

A frightened Nandi Bear bolted out of the bushes. It was completely engulfed in flames. The cryptid collided with the two pirates, and fell on top of them, setting them on fire. Butros and Tarik bolted past the screaming men, never once looking back.

Allen raised his arms above his head and brought them down by his sides, the motion signaling the vegetation ahead to spread apart like a curtain parting for a stage performance. The beach was straight ahead.

"We made it," Jack yelled.

Miguel stepped out onto the black sand. "Can't say the same for our ride."

Laney saw the launch; battered to pieces by the storm and half buried in the sand.

"Look over there," Miguel shouted.

Two long-range helicopters were flying low over the ocean. One aircraft banked toward the Dark Horizon. The chopper hovered over the ship's main deck. Rappel ropes were cast down. Military-types slid down, firing their weapons at the pirates below.

The other helicopter swooped for the island, its landing skids skimming the incoming wave tops as it came in for a soft landing on the beach.

Laney's heart dropped when she saw Wilde Enterprises stenciled on the fuselage. "Oh my God, Allen."

The side door slid open. Two commandos jumped down on the sand with Russian-made AA-12 Atchisson assault shotguns with round drum magazines like a gangster's Thompson submachine gun.

Jack and Miguel put up their hands.

Butros and Tarik made the mistake of pointing their guns at the men.

The elite specialists didn't hesitate and opened fire with their fully automatic 300 rounds per minute shotguns designed for extreme accuracy, as the weapons had no recoil.

Butros and Tarik flailed spasmodically, their bodies blown apart into a thousand fragments, bloody gore slapping the sand like raining-down dead fish. The commandos took a moment to swap out their magazines.

Laney saw another man appear in the helicopter's open hatchway.

It was Ivan Connors.

"Allen, run!"

Laney and Allen raced back into the jungle inferno.

36

PLEASURE CRUISE

Star rode the thermals, circling over the sinking island.

Lava continued to flow down the torched landscape to the swiftly shrinking shoreline. Plumes of steam rose from the surrounding ocean. Like an enormous ship going under, the molten rock submerged in a bubbling billow of escaping gases. The cloud of volcanic ash drifted up with the sea breeze dissipating in the fluffy white cumulous clouds. The island was no more.

The tern watched the ship and the two tiny flying dots disappear over the horizon.

All around was blue sky and ocean with no sign of land in sight, which didn't alarm Star. Since its kinship with Allen, the bird's senses, though previously keen, had become phenomenonally acute. The trigeminal nerve between its brain and beak, which served as an internal global positioning system, was working at inconceivable levels.

Star decided on a course after taking an imprint from the sun then dove, gliding over the flat ocean like a flying fish. It traveled this way for miles before lighting down on a bamboo railing.

"Well, hello," Laney said. She reached over, stroking the bird's damp variegated feathers. She was reclining in a rattan chair, wearing a straw hat.

She could feel the sun's heat on her legs. Looking up, she saw an elephant palm leaf had partially dislodged from the bamboo rafter above her head, allowing the sun to beat through. She stood, planting her feet firmly on the softly rolling raft. She stretched her hands up and pulled the leaf back in place.

"I would have done that." Allen stepped across the balsa log flooring lashed together with hemp rope; his self-made vessel organically constructed by his ability to generate any plant life of his choosing. Even the sail on the single mast was made of woven fronds. He sat down in the high back rattan chair next to Laney to soak up some sun and get an energy boost.

Star flittered off the railing and perched on the top of Allen's chair.

Laney looked up and smiled at the bird. "You better not poop on Allen's head."

"Like I'd really care." Allen reached under the bamboo railing. He pulled up a string of kelp with a small sea bass trapped in the aquatic plant. He fused his forefinger and middle finger together on his right hand into the shape of a razor-sharp saw palmetto and filleted the fish. He cut it in small pieces and tightly wrapped each one in a roll of seaweed. He put them on a leaf platter, placing it on the wicker table between their chairs.

"Thank you, Allen." Laney stared at the raw fish.

"What's wrong? You love sushi."

"I do. Just not for every meal." Laney glanced up at Star pacing on the back of Allen's chair.

"You would eat our pet?"

"No, Allen. I'd just like to change it up. Or have you forgotten since you no longer crave real food?"

"Sunlight and water; I'm a happy man." Allen stared at the tiny blades of sedge shimmering in the sunlight, growing from his pores on his green arms and hands. "Jesus, Laney. What happens now?"

"It's a big ocean. We'll figure it out." Laney picked up a sushi roll and popped it in her mouth.

Allen opened his hand, revealing a miniature magenta bouquet sprouting from his palm. "I love you, Laney."

Laney leaned over and gave her husband a kiss. "And I will always love you, Allen Moss."

37

PACIFIC NORTHWEST

THREE WEEKS LATER...

For the past five days, Jack and Miguel had been backpacking deeper and deeper into the conifer forest of towering Douglas-firs and western hemlocks; trekking into wilderness never before explored. Morning dew dripped from their slickers as they marched through the waist-high mist. Their boots crunched over hardpacked snow that had fallen the night before, vapor escaping their mouths in the frosty air with each labored breath.

"I need a minute," Jack called out to Miguel a few feet ahead.

Miguel stopped and turned. "You can't be tired. It's only been an hour."

"I got something in my boot." Jack slipped off his backpack, dropping it on the ground. He sat down on a log. He untied the laces and slipped off his boot. Reaching inside he felt around. "Here it is." He showed Miguel the culprit of his discomfort, a small pebble, and then tossed it into a clump of ferns.

Jack smoothed out his sock and put his boot back on. He got up, grabbed his backpack, and hoisted the straps over his shoulders.

They continued hiking between the massive trees on a migratory path flattened by deer and moose in search of food. The mountain air smelled of pine needles and humus soil. Up in the far away branches, eagles screeched, their high-pitched shrieks echoing in the dense forest.

The low-lying fog was beginning to thin out, the vaporous moisture now only ankle-deep. Miguel stopped when they came to a talus of boulders stretching forty feet up a rise to a hilltop of what seemed to be endless forest. He gazed down at a depression at the base of the rock partially concealed in the cloying mist.

Jack came up beside him and stared down at the dark hollow. "Could be a hibernation cave."

"I'm going to check it out." Miguel removed his backpack and leaned it against a tree. He took out his flashlight. He was about to start down when Jack asked, "Not taking your gun?"

"If I get in any trouble I'll give you a holler." Miguel had chosen not to wear his shoulder rig, as it was cumbersome and chafed his skin with the added pressure of the overlaying straps of his backpack. It was easier to stow and access his .357 Desert Eagle from an outer side pocket on his bag.

Jack had a similar problem; the wide waist belt on his backpack didn't ride correctly on his hips because of his gun belt. As the weight of the pack wasn't properly distributed, hauling the forty-pound pack began to put a strain on his back. His Colt was inside a pouch under his rolled up sleeping bag attached with a bungee cord.

Not having their guns at their fingertips hadn't seemed necessary. The wildlife they encountered was either nervous deer or small frightened animals scampering in the bushes. The most threatening varmint they encountered had been a badger blocking the trail, but it eventually backed off and retreated into its burrow.

Miguel stepped down the slope, disappearing into the fog, his boots clomping on a granite floor as he entered the cave.

Jack slipped off his backpack, dumping the heavy bag on the ground. He rolled his shoulders to get the kinks out. Stretching his arms away from his sides, he caught his right sleeve on a ragged branch. Not wanting to tear his shirt, he gently pried the fabric from the limb.

A swath of gray hair with a small piece of skin hung off the branch.

"Well, what do you know?" Jack took a clear plastic bag out of a side pocket on his backpack. He plucked the matted tuft from the twig and placed it inside the bag. He stuffed it inside his shirt pocket.

Jack looked down. The tule fog was gone. He saw a giant footprint on the snow-packed ground.

He placed his boot inside the depression. The imprint was twice the size of his foot. He saw another footprint, then another; sloping down to where Miguel had just gone.

"Oh, crap!" Jack rushed over to the edge of the rocks and called out, "Miguel, get the hell out of there!"

A loud roar boomed inside the cave.

Miguel came running out. He clawed his way up the rocky slope. "Jack, run!"

Jack tossed Miguel's backpack to his friend, grabbing his own. Neither had time to put them on properly, hauling them by the straps as they ran.

Sneaking a peek over his shoulder, Jack saw the beast charging over the crest of the incline. It had to be eight feet tall, covered with shaggy gray hair; arms lanky like a primate, thick lumbering legs with enormous feet. A menacingly powerful 600-pound animal but not particularly fast.

Jack and Miguel raced through the forest, the oafish creature in pursuit, stomping through the trees. Jack wanted desperately to dump his burdensome pack to quicken his pace, but that would mean abandoning his gun and supplies, lessening his chances of survival and getting out of the forest alive. They kept running for what seemed an eternity, not stopping until they couldn't take another step and collapsed to the ground.

Jack fumbled in his pack. He pulled out his revolver expecting at any second the creature would come crashing down the path to maul them to death.

The only sound he heard was the soft rustling of the branches.

"My God, I was so close to getting a sample of that thing," Miguel said, catching his breath.

Jack reached inside his shirt pocket. He showed Miguel the clear plastic bag with the tuft of hair. "No worries. I got us covered."

"Where the hell did you get that?"

"Off a tree."

"You mean, while I was down there almost getting my head ripped off."

"Hey, how did I know?" Jack stood. He strapped on his backpack. He kept his revolver handy. "Come on, let's go home."

38

REVEALED

Lucas Finder walked into the massive hangar being used to retrofit an entire fleet of transport trucks. Metal workers were busily building the enormous cages on the flatbed trailers that would later be covered with heavy-duty tarps to conceal the cargo so as not to attract unwanted attention.

He donned a pair of protective lens safety glasses to watch a welder, wearing a full-face helmet and heavy leather gloves, spot-weld joints with an oxyacetylene torch. The air was thick with toxic smoke drifting from the flying sparks. Lucas pulled out his clipboard tucked under his arm. He made a special note to get more circulating fans.

After completing his rounds in the hangar, Lucas set out across the compound to a nondescript windowless three-story building that looked like a large waterfront warehouse from the outside. Two security guards armed with Uzi pistols stood on either side of the fortified metal entry door.

"Afternoon, Mr. Finder," the tall guard greeted.

"Henry." Lucas acknowledged the other man. "Bill."

Lucas slipped his passkey into the reader. The heavy locks disengaged with a loud *thunk*. The pneumatic door swung open. He stepped through, the impenetrable door clunking behind him.

He walked down a short corridor towards another closed door where a guard was posted wearing a Glock sidearm. As Lucas didn't recognize the man, he flashed his Wilde Enterprises top clearance employee badge. The guard nodded and motioned for Lucas to swipe his passkey. The automatic door opened with a *swish* and Lucas went in.

A hallway led into a small maze of cubicles reserved for the lab assistants and supporting technicians. Large pane windows and glass doors separated the outer offices utilized by various scientific team members.

Lucas tapped on the glass door with the name plaque: Professor Nora Howard, M.D, Ph.D. An attractive woman in a white lab coat looked up from her desk. She gave Lucas a guarded smile and motioned for him to enter.

As soon as he came into her office, he saw she wasn't alone. "Hello, Cam."

The young man in the gray uniform half stood from his seat to acknowledge Lucas. Cam Morgan was one of a dozen animal caretakers maintaining the facility. He had a worried look on his face.

"Anything I should know about?" Lucas asked. As project manager of Wilde Enterprises, he had to be privy to every aspect pertaining to all of his boss' business ventures, especially billionaire Carter Wilde's latest all-time pet project.

Nora sat back from her desk. "There's a problem with the bats."

"The ones you bioengineered from the tooth?"

"That's right."

"What's wrong with them?"

"Cam, you want to tell Mr. Finder?"

"It was my fault really. I tried to introduce a youngster too early to the adults."

"What happened?"

"They ate it."

"You mean these things are cannibalistic?"

Nora looked at Lucas. "They don't seem to bond well. Their imprinting has been distorted in the lab somewhere along the way. I'll work on it."

"What about McCabe? Does he know about this?" Dr. Joel McCabe was head geneticist of the program.

"He might. You know him. He's not one for sharing."

"Yeah, he's not exactly a team player but he's the best at what he does."

Nora smiled at Cam. "Next time, please check with me first."

"I will. Thanks, Professor Howard." Cam got up from his seat and left the office.

Lucas remained standing at the door. "Mind if I take a peek?"

"No, not at all." Nora stood up from her desk.

As they were leaving Nora's office, they heard a loud commotion from another office down the hall. A bearded man in a white lab coat was yelling at a man in a three-piece business suit.

"Who's that with Dr. McCabe?" Nora asked Lucas.

"One of the corporate lawyers."

They watched as the attorney strode out of Dr. McCabe's office. In a fit of anger, McCabe snatched up a microscope from his desk and smashed it on the floor.

"Son of a bitch," Lucas groaned. "That was a two-thousand dollar piece of equipment. That's definitely coming out of his budget." He made a note of it on a sheet on his clipboard.

Nora led the way into the laboratory. She stopped at a workbench and placed a clear plastic bag containing a swath of gray hair on the tabletop.

"What's that going to be?" Lucas asked.

"Hopefully, a Bigfoot."

"Where was that found?"

"British Columbia."

"So how many teams do you have out there?"

"Only the one. Jack Tremens and Miguel Walla."

"Do they know about the other teams?"

"That they're all dead? No. I was afraid if they knew they wouldn't participate. I know that sounds callous."

"How is your mother?"

"She has her good days and bad."

"It's good the company's picking up the medical bills. I understand that medication she's on is pretty expensive."

"Five-hundred thousand dollars a year. Which is why I can't let anyone jeopardize this project. If Carter Wilde doesn't see positive results, he'll cut the funding, and I'm out of a job."

Lucas followed Nora over to a door. She used her keycard and swiped it down the reader. The moment the door began to automatically open, Lucas heard a cacophony of animal and bird sounds he would expect in a jungle teeming with wildlife.

As he stepped into the cavernous room, he saw a giant black panther as big as a horse, pacing back and forth in a cage. Birds the size of airplane gliders perched on swings in a three-story tall aviary. A blue tiger took one look at Lucas and snarled, baring its long fangs. Two fifteen-feet long monitor lizards flicked their tongues. A wild ape-man twice his height gaped down at him.

Lucas looked around at the many amazing creatures occupying the other enclosures once believed to be legends and myths created by a God-like myriad of genetics tampering to appease the idiosyncratic Carter Wilde in making his boyhood dream come true...CRYPTID ZOO.

ACKNOWLEDGEMENTS

I would like to thank Gary Lucas and the wonderful people working with Severed Press that helped with this book. Special thanks as always to Nichola Meaburn for her keen eye. It's truly amazing how folks we may never meet and who live in the most incredible places in the world can truly enrich our lives. And I would especially like to thank my daughter and faithful beta reader, Genene Griffiths Ortiz, for making this so much fun and sharing these bizarre and incredible journeys.

ABOUT THE AUTHOR

Gerry Griffiths lives in San Jose, California, with his family and their five rescue dogs and a cat. He is a Horror Writers Association member and has over thirty published short stories in various anthologies and magazines, as well as a short story collection entitled *Creatures*. He is also the author of *Silurid, The Beasts of Stoneclad Mountain, Down From Beast Mountain, Terror Mountain, Cryptid Island* and *Cryptid Zoo (Cryptid Zoo series Book 1)* as well as *Death Crawlers* and the follow-up standalone novels, *Deep in the Jungle, The Next World,* and *Battleground Earth,* all published by Severed Press.

CHECK OUT OTHER GREAT CRYPTID NOVELS

BIGFOOT WAR
by Eric S. Brown

Now a feature film from Origin Releasing. For the first time ever, all three core books of the Bigfoot War series have been collected into a single tome of Sasquatch Apocalypse horror. Remastered and reedited this book chronicles the original war between man and beast from the initial battles in Babblecreek through the apocalypse to the wastelands of a dark future world where Sasquatch reigns supreme and mankind struggles to survive. If you think you've experienced Bigfoot Horror before, think again. Bigfoot War sets the bar for the genre and will leave you praying that you never have to go into the woods again.

CRYPTID ZOO
by Gerry Griffiths

As a child, rare and unusual animals, especially cryptid creatures, always fascinated Carter Wilde.

Now that he's an eccentric billionaire and runs the largest conglomerate of high-tech companies all over the world, he can finally achieve his wildest dream of building the most incredible theme park ever conceived on the planet...CRYPTID ZOO.

Even though there have been apparent problems with the project, Wilde still decides to send some of his marketing employees and their families on a forced vacation to assess the theme park in preparation for Opening Day.

Nick Wells and his family are some of those chosen and are about to embark on what will become the most terror-filled weekend of their lives—praying they survive.

STEP RIGHT UP AND GET YOUR FREE PASS...

TO CRYPTID ZOO

CHECK OUT OTHER GREAT BIGFOOT NOVELS

THE BEASTS OF STONECLAD MOUNTAIN by Gerry Griffiths

Clay Morgan is overjoyed when he is offered a place to live in a remote wilderness at the base of a notorious mountain. Locals say there are Bigfoot living high up in the dense mountainous forest. Clay is skeptic at first and thinks it's nothing more than tall tales.

But soon Clay becomes a believer when giant creatures invade his new home and snatch his baby boy, Casey.

Now, Clay and his wife, Mia, must rescue their son with the help of Clay's uncle and his dog, a journey up the foreboding mountain that will take them into an unimaginable world...straight into hell!

BIGFOOT AWAKENED by Alex Laybourne

A weekend away with friends was supposed to be fun. One last chance for Jamie to blow off some steam before she leaves for college, but when the group make a wrong turn, fun is the last thing they find.

From the moment they pass through a small rural town they are being hunted by whatever abominations live in the woods.

Yet, as the beasts attack and the truth is revealed, they learn that despite everything, man still remains the most terrifying evil of them all.

CHECK OUT OTHER GREAT CRYPTID NOVELS

SWAMP MONSTER MASSACRE by Hunter Shea

The swamp belongs to them. Humans are only prey. Deep in the overgrown swamps of Florida, where humans rarely dare to enter, lives a race of creatures long thought to be only the stuff of legend. They walk upright but are stronger, taller and more brutal than any man. And when a small boat of tourists, held captive by a fleeing criminal, accidentally kills one of the swamp dwellers' young, the creatures are filled with a terrifyingly human emotion—a merciless lust for vengeance that will paint the trees red with blood.

TERROR MOUNTAIN by Gerry Griffiths

When Marcus Pike inherits his grandfather's farm and moves his family out to the country, he has no idea there's an unholy terror running rampant about the mountainous farming community. Sheriff Avery Anderson has seen the heinous carnage and the mutilated bodies. He's also seen the giant footprints left in the snow—Bigfoot tracks. Meanwhile, Cole Wagner, and his wife, Kate, are prospecting their gold claim farther up the valley, unaware of the impending dangers lurking in the woods as an early winter storm sets in. Soon the snowy countryside will run red with blood on TERROR MOUNTAIN.

Made in the USA
Middletown, DE
25 November 2020